Chronicling the Days

Dispatches from a Pandemic

ESSENTIAL ANTHOLOGIES SERIES 15

Canadä

ONTARIO ARTS COUNCIL
CONSEIL DES ARTS DE L'ONTARIO
an Ontario government agency
un organisme du gouvernement de l'Ontario

Canada Council   Conseil des arts
for the Arts   du Canada

Guernica Editions Inc. acknowledges the support of
the Canada Council for the Arts and the Ontario Arts Council.
The Ontario Arts Council is an agency of the Government of Ontario.
We acknowledge the financial support of the Government of Canada.

Chronicling the Days

Dispatches from a Pandemic

EDITED BY
**Linda M. Morra &
Marianne Ackerman**

**GUERNICA
EDITIONS**
TORONTO · CHICAGO · BUFFALO · LANCASTER (U.K.)
2021

Michael Mirolla & Connie McParland, general editors
Linda M. Morra & Marianne Ackerman, editors
Cover and interior design: Rafael Chimicatti
Guernica Editions Inc.
287 Templemead Drive, Hamilton (ON), Canada L8W 2W4
2250 Military Road, Tonawanda, N.Y. 14150-6000 U.S.A.
www.guernicaeditions.com

Distributors:
Independent Publishers Group (IPG)
600 North Pulaski Road, Chicago IL 60624
University of Toronto Press Distribution,
5201 Dufferin Street, Toronto (ON), Canada M3H 5T8
Gazelle Book Services, White Cross Mills
High Town, Lancaster LA1 4XS U.K.

First edition.
Printed in Canada.

Legal Deposit – First Quarter
Library of Congress Catalog Card Number: 2020946592
Library and Archives Canada Cataloguing in Publication
Title: Chronicling the days : dispatches from a pandemic
edited by Linda M. Morra & Marianne Ackerman.
Names: Morra, Linda M., editor. | Ackerman, Marianne, editor.
Quebec Writers' Federation.
Description: First edition. | Series statement: Essential anthologies series ; 15
Collection of pieces submitted to Chronicling the days,
a Quebec Writers' Federation community writing project.
Identifiers: Canadiana (print) 20200341138 | Canadiana (ebook)
20200341960 | ISBN 9781771836579 (softcover)
ISBN 9781771836586 (EPUB) | ISBN 9781771836593 (Kindle)
Subjects: LCSH: COVID-19 (Disease)—Québec (Province)—Anecdotes.
LCSH: Epidemics—Québec (Province)—Anecdotes. | LCSH: Quarantine—
Québec (Province)—Anecdotes. | CSH: Authors, Canadian (English)—
Québec (Province)—Anecdotes. | LCGFT: Anecdotes.
Classification: LCC RA644.C67 C47 2021 | DDC 362.1962/414—dc23

For Joel Yanofsky
(26 September 1955 – 23 December 2020)
"The heart and soul of Montreal's literary community"

—Mark Abley

Contents

· · · · · · · · ·

Prelude
Susan Doherty, 11

The Days

Prelude

· · · · · · · ·

SUSAN DOHERTY

Wednesday, March 11, 2020: the day COVID-19 went from a global emergency to a pandemic. Flights were cancelled, as Prime Minister Trudeau ordered Canadians to return home. Inevitably, some citizens would be stranded as international borders were closing by the hour. An important Texas film festival, SXSW 2020, had already cancelled its annual event, after worried headliners began to pull out—the beginning of the end for so many live performances around the world. There was even talk the Olympics might be postponed! That week, we were all asked to stop, stand still, and keep six feet apart—the new concept of social distancing meant to prevent the spread of the virus. Canadians returning from abroad were told to quarantine. We experienced a false sense of security as the Director-General of the WHO tried to reassure us this would be the first pandemic in history that could be controlled. We were not at the mercy of the virus.

On that fateful day in March, I was in London having lunch with the man who had saved my life—my British stem cell donor, William—and his husband, Michael. Like most joyous reunions, it featured hugging and kissing, and plenty of clinking of glasses. The following day, he was rushed to hospital by ambulance with breathing issues. He had lost his sense of taste and smell, symptoms as yet unidentified with coronavirus. He was not tested. There were no tests. Prime Minister Boris Johnson had the mistaken idea that transmission was containable in the UK, underestimating the threat, even though Italy and Spain were confronting a rising national crisis of deathly contagion.

I was home in Montreal, when William called me in a panic. Had I fallen ill? I drove to a test site near Place-des-Arts and was ushered into a white tent by a police officer. Six days later, I received an email: "*Négatif.*" I had already rationalized that a God who sent William Ashby-Hall to save my life would not send the same man to kill me.

As March turned into April, William recovered, but the world-wide cases continued to surge, dealing an oxygen-sucking blow to our creativity. The perilous unknown momentarily overtook our need to write stories. Our attention was diverted to the untenable situation of people dying alone or saying goodbye through mobile devices. The loneliness of death was a relative newcomer in our collective consciousness. Nothing seemed more important than senior care homes decimated, or tourist meccas like New York City and Venice turned into ghost towns, or freezer trucks parked outside hospitals filling up with body bags too numerous to be sent to funeral homes. The ghastly images side-swept our voices. We stayed home, baked bread, home-schooled our children, sat transfixed by Crave and Netflix. We shared memes that made us laugh. Zoom became a new verb.

Had Mother Nature called us to account for our disregard of the oceans, the skies, our excessive use of fossil fuels? Suddenly, the Himalayas were visible from great distances. There was a silver lining, we said. Our planet might be in recovery for the next generation.

We were asked to distinguish between essential, necessary, and expendable. Alcohol was considered essential, but crossing the border to be at the birth of a first child was not. Thankfully nurses, cashiers, orderlies, shelf re-stockers, and medical teams were—and are—essential. The material world has taken a back seat to the essential, illuminating what is expendable and what isn't, including our human possessions.

In the midst of surging COVID cases, George Floyd's death from traumatic asphyxia gripped America, then the entire world. His brutal murder by police unleashed an outcry about human rights that will reverberate for decades. We can thank the pandemic for this forward propulsion toward greater respect for such rights.

Public events, literary readings, award ceremonies, book fairs, workshops, lectures, and residency-scholarships were cancelled. Unemployment numbers entered the stratosphere. Yet history has shown that humanity has a capacity for great resilience. Everyone suffers. It's how we react to suffering that dictates the outcome. Inch by inch, we returned to the business of being writers, editors, and publishers, caretakers of our stories.

Perhaps we'll never again shake hands or greet each other with a casual embrace, but a writer's need to remember and record humanity will ensure we continue to touch many others with the power of our words.

The Days

"What Are Days For?"

ARIELA FREEDMAN

· · · · · · · ·

"What are days for?"
This line begins a Philip Larkin poem that I first read on the New York subway, sandwiched between ads for cosmetic surgery and real estate brokers. The question has been on my mind over these disrupted, strange, static weeks.

This morning, I woke up a little after 6 am. I was dreaming that we drove down an underpass and into an ocean. But we didn't drown; when I woke up, my dream self was still trying to figure out how to push the car back onto dry land. Not subtle, my unconscious. Not drowning yet, but waving.

I live in a semi-detached house with a yard. I have never been so conscious of the luxuries of outdoor space and different rooms. We are four, and we have each found our level: my teenage boys are upstairs in their respective rooms, my husband works from the basement, and I have squatted the living room, which has a big window and a view of the park across the street. My neighbour's fence was removed over the winter, so I can see her garden from my back porch. Her brother has been in the hospital with COVID-19 for a week. He was just released from the ICU. I offer her eggs. Our interactions feel so archaic these days—small gestures of care across the yard.

I'm still teaching, finishing my term, and I'm preparing for Passover, which has always felt like a period of isolation anyway. I can't believe how apt a time it is to teach Michel Foucault and his take on quarantine and disciplined bodies, and the way states of exception become new norms. I edit a GIF of Bart Simpson at the blackboard to read: "I will wash my hands for twenty seconds one hundred times a day"—and add it to my presentation.

What are days for? The same old things, although they feel different. Preparing classes, and taking walks, and reading too much news, and doing yoga. Making bread, god help us all. My current writing project, which I began a year ago, has me researching the Spanish Flu, and it is disconcerting to see the same crisis at a hundred-year remove. Ads for powders that claim to strengthen the body against the flu, for phonograph machines because the concert halls are closed.

Days are where we live, Larkin says, and some snarky Jewish vaudeville voice from my ancestral past says: *You call that living*? Still: we saw crocuses on our walk this morning. I heard a falcon's cry from a distance and am hoping Polly and Algo have returned to the church beside the park, where they have nested for the last few years. I am looking for the small pleasures: the green velvet of moss on brick, and how loud the birds sound in the quiet city. "Days are to be happy in," Larkin writes, whose usual note is misery (I can relate). "Where can we live but days?"

In the Grip of the Nightmare

GEOFFREY EDWARDS

· · · · · · · · ·

The nightmare still has its hold on me as I awaken. The dark is all around, and I find myself thinking, it is a time of ending. It takes me more than an hour to calm the rapid heartbeat, to find the state of quiet acceptance that allows me to sleep again.

I have nothing urgent to do in the morning. No places to go, even if I wanted to—which I do. I hope to lose some weight, but it still fluctuates up and down, even though I pace my eating. A friend has been delivering groceries, but I hold off asking her each time, until I'm almost out of everything. I am conscious that buying groceries has become an ordeal, but my friends are the very people who have convinced me that I am at risk. Whenever I get a cold, it takes me weeks to shake it off, and usually requires a visit to the doctor and a prescription for antibiotics. They say, however, that antibiotics don't help with the coronavirus. And I read that high blood pressure adds to the risk.

Not the retirement I had in mind, although I also consider myself extremely lucky. My income is guaranteed, at least for a while, until the pension funds bottom out. Unlike my former colleagues at the university, I have largely quiet days, while they are working at a frantic pace, often from early in the morning until late at night, and all weekend, trying to stay on top of the demands of online classes that had to be created out of nothing.

My writing is going well, when I can find the peace of mind to work on it. I finished the revisions on one manuscript and have moved onto another that needs to be tidied up. I still take the time to read the news for an hour or more: *The Guardian*, *The New York*

Times, Radio-Canada, and CBC, in that order. The American situation is catastrophic; I grieve for my American friends. I speak online with a writer friend in New York every week, and wonder if he will still be there from one week to the next. But neither is our situation in Canada without worries.

I work with an innovation firm that is looking into post-COVID actions, straddling the world of worthy causes with the requirements of a viable business plan. Still, at least we are thinking about what that world will be like, and how we could make it better. As a former researcher, this reconciles me to being sidelined through retirement.

However, I am also aware that the lack of social contact is beginning to wear. I am not prone to depression, but I could see how that might be a looming problem in these times. And if I'm thinking that, what of others, not so lucky as I? No wonder I have nightmares.

Plenty of Food for Thought

GINA ROITMAN

. . . .

Today was our first day out after a two-week quarantine following a complicated and harrowing return from Europe. But that's another story. We're accustomed to isolation and working from home, as we live in the Lower Laurentians; that has not been a hardship. But we came back to Canada after five weeks in Spain and France, to a larder I had allowed to go bare before leaving.

This morning, we could finally shop for groceries, but we had to choose between Costco in Saint-Jérôme or Bourassa, a wholesale grocer in Saint-Sauveur. Although I'm not a fan, we opted for Costco, because it's well stocked and, more importantly, massive, making social distancing easier.

Food and its future availability are of great concern to Axel. His thinking is that with immigrant farm workers becoming sick and unable to receive medical assistance, harvesting the crops this summer will be difficult. And when fall comes along, who will seed the fields?

Costco opens at 10 am. We arrived at 10.10 am and were stunned to find the line stretching around the building, and around the huge block. We stood in the rain for almost an hour before being admitted inside, but kudos to the company for being well organized. The method of controlling entry was very efficient; as we drew closer to the front door, we were given a sanitized cart.

I was wearing latex gloves and one of the masks we made from an instructive YouTube video that proved quite effective. While standing in the rain, the mask kept me warm but fogged up my glasses. Once in, it took two hours to go up and down every aisle, checking my list (checking it twice) and still adding items I had forgotten to include.

That's the thing about Costco and the fear of a future shortage: Everything looks like it's under a MUST HAVE sign. Expecting a tally of about $300, I was rocked back on my heels when the register read $500. The cash checkout, however, was highly organized with Plexiglas shields for the cashiers, no bags or boxes: everything out of the shopping cart, scanned, then back into the cart. I had no time to register my shock.

There's a Mondou next to the Costco and, before heading home, I insisted that we stop to buy what I call bird seed and Axel calls squirrel food. After all, if I'm not leaving the house until the larder is once again almost bare, keeping company with the birds and squirrels is better than watching the news.

Spending Time in My Head

ROMY SHILLER

· · · · · · · · ·

These days I spend a lot of time in my head, and drinking coffee. I'm so friggin' bored. I keep thinking of the movie *Groundhog Day*, and I feel guilty. In the movie, Rita says to Phil (the Bill Murray character): "So, this is what you do with eternity." I think he was stuffing pastries into his mouth at the time. He ends up learning to play an instrument, reading something obviously intellectual, and helping strangers. Even though every day is the same, he chooses to be productive. Yup, not me. I think that what I do or don't do is the equivalent of stuffing pastries into my mouth.

Oh yeah, I was disabled from brain surgery in 2003. Physical distance is pretty much impossible for me. My caregivers, who are considered an essential service, have to transfer me to a toilet, bath, or bed. This involves very close body contact. They take necessary precautions, but they also all live with people whose habits are unknown to me, so I get extremely anxious. If I get the infection and it travels to my brain I'm doomed, because I have a working shunt. There is so much we don't know about this coronavirus. Does it travel in the body? No wonder I am not productive; the worry is exhausting.

Also, the idea of self-isolation is very different for me. I am never alone. I do rely on coffee shops, restaurants, malls, physiotherapy, and so on being open to get me out of here. Otherwise, I stay home and write pop-culture reviews; in that respect, I have consistency. *I do* miss going out to movie theatres.

My caregiver went to the pharmacy for me today. Momentary privacy. Bliss.

At least I get to talk to different people during the week, but they are not friends or family or my kids. People complain about their jobs. I am sympathetic to their plight, but I AM a job.

Emma is with me today. We are completely irreverent about disability. Even though most people would be so offended by our humour, I am grateful for it, especially since it feels like I'm living in the Zombie Apocalypse. Today, she inadvertently held my calf too tight while putting on my slipper. Yes, I even need help getting dressed. We call physical accidents "Fight Club." So when I say "ouch," it's a funny moment.

I am usually alone in my head, but now my thoughts have company. Anxiety and worry are my children who interrupt work and need attention. The thing is, I can't give them a colouring book or school assignments to make them behave.

My physicality usually constrains movement, but this is exacerbated by the pandemic. I often think of the film *Titanic*. The pandemic feels like the ship is going down, but today the sun is shining, and I'll get fresh air.

Smile—and Read the Fine Print

LISANNE GAMELIN

. . . .

Whether or not your financial institution is doing well by you, you need them right now, and that's where most of my days in this weird post-apocalyptic world are being spent. Inside that belly. I still know what day it is, because, by the end of the week, I want nothing to do with anyone anymore. Self-isolation on the weekend has become bliss.

Most of my days are spent on the phone, talking people down from ledges, trying to reassure them that their business isn't going to shit. Like everyone, I do not know the future, but I've got to keep it optimistic, one call after another. Have to pretend that I've got it under control. I can't panic or lose my temper. I've got to stay as cool as a cucumber.

I'm a business advisor at a financial institution, which is a fancy title for working in a call centre. In the past few weeks, you might have heard these numerous government announcements: Money. Money. Money. Money being injected everywhere! Woot!

People are starting to believe it's all for free.

Well, sorry to be the bearer of bad news, but they are still technically loans, and there are always strings attached. Read the fine print. And, after a few (short in my mind, but long for others) weeks since these daily announcements began, I'm starting to lose track of them.

Every day, I field calls, asking: "How can I get that 40K from Trudeau? What about that new 3K from Legault?"

Truth is this: We don't know yet.

But you keep calling. And we keep giving the same answer. Over and over.

We don't know yet. Especially if that announcement was made fifteen minutes ago. Sorry.

And then, usually, you follow with a sigh of desperation. You don't need to be loud—we hear you.

We hear it all. We feel your frustration. We share it. After a little while, I can even hear the eye rolls over the phone.

Growing up in French, I used to watch *Astérix* often, especially *Les 12 travaux d'Astérix*. In that 1976 French cartoon classic, Astérix and Obélix have to go through twelve tasks, much like Hercules. My favourite task had always been "la maison qui rend fou," a.k.a. "the bureaucratic house driving you nuts." I've always found that task to be the funniest. Astérix eventually turns the system against itself, breaking the vicious cycle of finding the infamous permit A38. I'd never realized how tough it would be to work in that crazy house, and that, eventually, yes, I would like nothing else but to kick back and install a swing in my office.

Channelling Camus from Another Plague

JIM UPTON

· · · · · · · ·

One of the ironies of life is that errors can prove rewarding rather than costly. I have in mind a tendency to buy too many books over a period of time and have most of them remain on bookshelves unread, despite the best of intentions. And then an unexpected occasion provides a chance to capitalize on a previous mistake.

As the coronavirus rolled over us, I noticed *The Plague* by Albert Camus on my bookshelf and began reading the novel, published in 1947, almost three-quarters of a century ago. It was not exactly a diversion, but it did remind me of how literature can provide a deeper understanding of ourselves and our world. Passages in the book were eerily contemporary. A few selections follow:

"There have been as many plagues in the world as there have been wars, yet plagues and wars always find people equally unprepared."

"The people of our town were no more guilty than anyone else, they merely forgot to be modest and thought that everything was still possible for them, which implied that pestilence was impossible. They continued with business, with making arrangements for travel and holding opinions. Why should they have thought about the plague, which negates the future, negates journeys and debate? They considered themselves free and no one will ever be free as long as there is plague, pestilence and famine."

"It may seem a ridiculous idea, but the only way to fight the plague is with decency."

"In the memory of those who have lived through them, the dreadful days of the plague do not seem like vast flames, cruel and magnificent, but rather like an endless trampling that flattened every-thing in its path."

"... the greatest suffering of the time, the most widespread and the deepest, was separation..."

"... the inhabitants of Oran... while they feel a deep need for warmth, which brings them together, at the same time cannot sur-render to it entirely because of the suspicion that keeps them apart. You know very well that you cannot trust your neighbour, that he is quite capable of giving you the plague without knowing it and taking advantage of your lowered guard to infect you."

"Speculators were involved and vital necessities, unobtainable on the ordinary market, were being offered at huge prices. Poor families consequently found themselves in a very difficult situation, while the rich lacked for practically nothing."

"All that a man could win in the game of plague and life was knowledge and memory."

"... one learns in the midst of such tribulations... that there is more in men to admire than to despise."

An Eerie Familiarity

LINDA M. MORRA

· · · · · · · · ·

There is hand gel at the door—a reminder to use it every time we
return. Several face masks are stashed inside the hallway closet,
collected from an earlier visit to the hospital just in case one of us
becomes ill. And no one—absolutely no one—thinks of dropping by
on a whim, even for a quick visit.

But these were the days that preceded the global pandemic and
calls for isolation; these were the days when my parents—first my
mother, then my father—were diagnosed with terminal cancer and
underwent chemotherapy.

There is something eerily familiar with what's happening now.
What's unfamiliar is that everyone feels it too: the anxiety, the dread.

That's what I was thinking, once again this morning, as I looked
out the window of my study. I sit at my desk and grade papers. This
part of my job hasn't changed much either—happily, I still have one,
even if how I teach has been radically altered.

About an hour later, I lose patience.

"That's it," I say to my partner.

I am brandishing scissors when he looks up from his book. I have
cut my own hair for the first time—about three inches shorter, just
below my ears.

"What do you think?"

"Nice," he says, without really looking. These are the civilities we
pay to each other, especially in close quarters. I am also still waving
around the scissors.

"Do you want me to cut yours?"

He glances at me again, looks at my hair dubiously. He has been murmuring about the length of his own.

"Maybe tomorrow." He continues reading.

For the rest of the day, I grade papers. And I think about how I used to wash and cut my mother's hair too, when she had any at all.

I still have hand gel at the door. I still have a couple of leftover face masks stashed in the closet.

I just don't have my parents.

Falling in Love Amid COVID-19

JIM OLWELL

· · · · ● · · · ·

I met Paule-Andrée online. We exchanged messages very easily and appreciatively thereafter for a week.

We seemed to be very attracted to each other.

We decided to meet in the Notre-Dame-des-Neiges Cemetery on the mountain yesterday, each taking our own car. Nobody else was there.

We walked for an hour, to and fro, without touching but talking, and had a couple of short chats on cold benches.

We returned to the cars and parked them, so that we could talk from our respective drivers' seats with windows half open.

I read her four poems from my book, *Pensions*, which she loved and by which she was touched. We were very sweet to each other.

We will go slowly, as there are no other choices.

I stay in the house all day, except for exercise walks; a wonderful Afro-Canadian francophone neighbour shops for me, on call. Another Quebecoise neighbour brings me brownies and carrot muffins.

Last night, I sent Paule-Andrée some thoughts about my feelings for her that I had originally intended to be just for myself.

She responded so beautifully, I can't believe it.

I am a Yeatsian romantic; I don't deny it. Sometimes, however, I get tripped up by it (and my own carnality).

But I think this is real.

She taught art to high school students as a career and has since travelled everywhere—I mean everywhere.

I am smitten. So is she.

We are romantics and enthusiasts, positive and sensual. We are seventy-four.

Ordinarily, I would encourage horizontal physical communication at this point—too early for the woman. Not this time. No choice but to go slow. But no sense of rejection.

My spring has sprung, and there's a wonderful fling to be flung.

But no touching, as we feel our relationship might better flourish if she and I stay alive on the way to forever.

PENNING THE PANDEMIC
Living and Writing in The Country

ANGELA LEUCK

. . . .

"We're thinking of moving to the country," I told mystery writer Louise Penny when I bumped into her at the Knowlton Literary Festival in 2010, adding that my husband and I weren't sure it was the right thing for our writing careers. Penny was enthusiastic: "Do it," she said, "while you can!" A few months later, we bought a 200-year-old farmhouse in the tiny hamlet of North Hatley.

For Penny, living in the country proved no hindrance to her career. Her depiction of the fictional village of Three Pines and the eccentric characters who inhabit it launched her to international success. Currently on the sixteenth volume of her Inspector Gamache series, she has sold over six million books worldwide.

Danish-born Anne Fortier lives in the village of North Hatley, nestled at the northern end of Lake Massawippi. Fortier is the author of the *The New York Times* bestseller *Juliet* as well as *The Lost Sisterhood,* and she is at work on her third novel.

Over the years, Quebec's Eastern Townships have been home to numerous literary figures: novelists Hugh MacLennan and Mordecai Richler; poets F.R. Scott, A.J.M. Smith, Ralph Gustafson, D.G. Jones, John Glassco, Richard Sommer, Susan Briscoe, and more.

I can hear my urban friends protest (although certainly less in these challenging times of the coronavirus!): what about the stimulation of the big city, schmoozing with other writers at workshops, book launches, or readings, and those all-important opportunities to rub shoulders with potential publishers? Surely you won't find that out in the sticks!

Yet, living in Hatley, where a local farmer's manure spreader is often a more common sight than a car or truck, I'm never bored. Outside my window is the natural world—verdant and ever-changing. But then, my writing is closely connected to nature and the seasons. One of my favourite writers is Saskatchewan-born Sharon Butala. Her acclaimed memoir *Perfection of the Morning* was inspired by her move from Saskatoon to a cattle ranch in the remote south-western corner of Saskatchewan. For my husband, too, writing is fed by his observations of nature on daily walks through fields and back roads.

It helps, of course, that we are in easy commuting distance to Montreal—less than two hours away. Early in her career, in the 1970s, Margaret Atwood and her husband Graeme Gibson lived on a farm near Alliston, Ontario, a convenient ninety minutes outside of Toronto.

In many ways, the internet has contributed to making distance far less important than it was.

I may live in a village of just 750 people, but I am connected online to a community of poets across Canada and around the world. Even if you choose to live in a ten-by-sixteen-foot cabin in the woods *à la* Thoreau (Brome area-writer Munira Judith Avinger did just this, as recounted in her 2012 memoir *The Cabin*), you can still enjoy high-speed internet as a result of the towers that have recently sprouted atop local peaks such as Mount Orford.

For me, the biggest surprise about the country is the number of writing groups—far more than knitting or quilting circles. Fiction and poetry writing groups abound. More specialized groups, such as memoir and storytelling at Uplands Museum in Lennoxville, science fiction at Literacy in Action in Lennoxville, and playwriting at Foss House in Eaton Corner, are free and open to new members. And this fall, the Quebec Writers' Federation is piloting a project to allow writers in remote areas to attend QWF workshops online.

Living in the country doesn't seem to stop local writers from attracting the attention of Canadian presses either. Milby poet Marjorie Bruhmuller is published by Ekstasis in Victoria and *Le petit nuage* of Ottawa. Down the road, our neighbour, QWF award-winning poet Ann Scowcroft, was published by Toronto's Brick Books. Kathleen McHale of Stanstead was published by Cormorant and Sutton poet Antony di Nardo has had books published by Ronsdale, Brick, and Exile.

If writers and writing flourish in the Townships, what about other rural areas of Quebec? I can only speak about regions with which I have personal experience: I had the great good fortune to spend six weeks as writer-in-residence at schools in Chevery and Harrington Harbour on the Lower North Shore, and also travelled to the Gaspésie to give several day-long blogging workshops. I'm happy to report that in both places I found equally vibrant and active writing communities.

Curses Make the Time Go By

NORA LORETO

• • • • • • • •

I have the most lucid dreams between 8:06 and 8:11 every morning. This morning, I was in what I imagine a cigar den might look like. There was a bar and low rise tables everywhere, made to seem even lower as a result of the high ceiling of the room. It was bright. There were people sitting closer than two metres together.

8:11 comes and the next dream that follows is barely a dream—it's more like intense thinking. Every day, I tell myself I'll get up earlier. Every day, I absorb every last inch of heat that my duvet, stolen by someone from the Château Frontenac at some point, still holds. I've never been to the Château Frontenac, but I imagine that it's wild to see it so empty.

It should be full of healthcare workers separated from their families, while they care for us through the pandemic.

My mornings are the most structured. Since *Le Soleil* stopped publishing its daily newspaper two weeks ago, I regret all those times my newspapers piled up because I didn't have a moment to read them. I fill my percolator to ten cups. Decaf. The kids are already busy with their grade-one prep workbooks. My presence breaks the idyllic scene.

I curse CBC radio's *The Current* for being too uncritical, too folksy, too bland, too hokey. It stays on until I find myself cursing the Prime Minister next, at 11:24 am, when he comes out only a little bit late. He tells us nothing about how the illness has advanced overnight. I think about working.

But I've been laid off. My tiny organization can't afford to pay me with our events cancelled. My semi-regular column is done too:

no more money. I don't have anything to do. I haven't gone this long without a paycheque since I was thirteen.

Radio Noon comes on. News out of Montreal reminds me that I certainly do not live there. It's fine. It could be more critical too. Everything could be more critical.

I play with the kids, spend too much time on Twitter, curse someone else online for something. I imagine going outside and then quickly unimagine it when I hear the interpreter introduce François Legault. I switch to Radio-Canada and sit on a step-stool staring at my phone for the next forty minutes.

The pandemic will change everything. While some are glued to the numbers of infections, my mind is fixed on what happens next. What will give birth to that new world? The battle over what kind of society will emerge has already begun.

Many measures intended to help will entrench inequality. Temporary measures will become permanent.

Tonight, I will drift into a dream while focusing on tomorrow's pot of coffee.

Captive's Log

APRIL FORD

· · · · · · · ·

Dear next Monday: I will conquer you. It's only Friday, so I have the whole weekend (and this evening) to prepare mentally. The first thing I'll do when I wake up Monday morning is write for two hours. Nothing will come between me and new words except for a shot of stovetop espresso, made with my single-cup Bialetti, which I should probably clean—like, really scrub—now that I have time. Usually, I just rinse it after each use, which, in light of the pandemic, seems kind of gross and maybe even dangerous. I really can't say, because Trudeau can't seem to say. Legault, though, he's pulling for us. (Never imagined myself saying *that*.)

I have already spotted a flaw in my plan for how to start next Monday: While I enjoy the *idea* of a stovetop espresso, I'm too sleepy in the morning to make good life choices. So instead of espresso, I make drip coffee, which I load with cream and sugar. This eventually causes me to have a sugar crash, which inevitably leaves me vulnerable to feelings of despair I can't describe as other than impossible to overcome. The despair only worsens if I try to focus on writing, or check the web for the most current information about the coronavirus. My only relief from this despair is a heavily-buttered croissant. And some Mini Babybels. This afternoon, I threw the remaining croissants and Mini Babybels in the garbage. It has come to this: If I can stop myself from picking through the garbage in a few hours, then I have met a goal I set for myself today. I have overcome a challenge. Surmounted an obstacle.

I AM A HORRIBLE PERSON. Wasteful in a time when conservation is critical. Even my cats are wasteful. Ernie has started refusing

40

her morning serving of Fancy Feast pâté. Nicolas has started flinging litter all over the place, just dives into the box and spins around like a nut. I wonder if they know the pandemic's outcome. Cats are supposed to be clairvoyant, after all. Maybe Netflix would be interested in a show about the unsung Joe Exotics of the animal kingdom. My elevator pitch would go something like:

Me: So I have an idea for a television series.
Producer: Oh?
Me: Yeah.
Producer: Can I hear it?
Me: I don't know, *can* you?
Producer: Really, April?
Me: Sorry. I'm a little grumpy these days. So it's a show about domestic cat-owners. We deserve a little fame, too, you know.
Producer: But what's it *about*? What's the big picture?
Me: What, are we in a fucking creative writing class all of a sudden?

There's nothing stopping me (except croissants and Mini Babybels) from seizing the day: sitting down to write for a couple of hours, and then trading the screen for some living-room yoga and a jaunt along the Lachine Canal. Next Monday will mark the start of my fourth week in isolation. Next week—starting with you, dear Monday—I'll get it right.

Fever... Sweats... Hallucinations

BYRON REMPEL

. . . .

April Fool's Day

Stores have installed large Plexiglas fronts on all their cashiers' posts. Probably some of these things will be that way for months or years; some will keep them always. Air-borne paranoia spreads through my village. There is a greeter at each Gate of Entry, dressed in a long, hooded black cape, and clutching a scythe. But it's all right. I enter with my Plague Doctor's mask, the pointed beak stuffed with aromatics and Trudeau's Essential Services Cannabis, all to protect me from the Pest.

There are families of crows come to protect our house. They say they are there to eat the peanuts in shells I toss out front every day, but I know the truth. They descend from a long line of tricksters, and that's the price they exact to bluster and waylay the killers that may blow our way.

A month of Sundays, in exchange for imminent death.

April 4, 2020

I wake up in the middle of the night, 3:39 am, with a splitting head-ache and my body sweating. It has finally arrived, the Virus, and now I must prepare to die. The fevers feed hallucinations. I swear I have woken in some apocalyptic future, where humans amble back and forth in their cubicles all day jacked into small hand-held devices, while outside a deadly enemy eats any who dare go shopping. I take Advil, lie back down, ready to face my fate—a slow, agonizing death. The day before, I wrote such a fatalistic metaphor that it has winged its way down to deal me my karma. I may never get back to sleep.

I'll probably have to take more pills to knock myself out, perhaps permanently. Here I will lie all night, until... I wake up at 9:01 am, refreshed, smiling, ready for the day.

It was only a hangover.

Who Would Have Thought...?

MURIEL GOLD POOLE

. . . .

Wednesdays are when I normally lead my writers' workshop in St Petersburg, Florida. Returning home due to COVID, I was forced to abandon it.

Not so fast. One of my writers (there are twenty of them) suggests I run the sessions from Montreal. Not through Zoom or Skype or FaceTime, G-d forbid. Luckily, a few of my participants are just as technologically challenged as I am, so we decide on email as the method of communication.

Normally, each week, near the end of the two-hour session, I give them a prompt, allotting ten minutes of writing that is followed by their readings and group feedback. I decide to try this practice online.

I give them the prompt: "Who would have thought..."—and the first one comes in almost immediately. Others follow, and the supportive comments from various members seem comforting, particularly at this time of isolation.

No sooner have I written my own contribution than the telephone rings. It is somewhat of a shock to discover that a family member has died, by virtue of medical assistance. Naturally, I want to write to the family, but they request no condolences. So I decide to write a story focused on the deceased. It is not easy and takes longer than expected, partly because my computer will not cooperate.

Meanwhile, my husband Ronald is online trying to order food; it is a challenge. In fact, it is frustrating because, after we complete the order, the computer screen requests that we "Choose a Time Slot," but, when we do, it indicates that "No Time Slot is Available." Not that we are on the verge of starvation. When we arrived home the previous week, my son, Glenn, realizing that our larder was empty, sprang into action and instructed his close friends, Richard and Ronda, to shop for us. At 9 am the next morning, bags of groceries arrived at our door, and rigorous washing of every item followed.

It is Day Fourteen of our quarantine, and the next challenge—how to use a communal laundry facility during a pandemic—begins later today. On with the masks, the gloves, and the antiseptic cleaners.

A knock at the door—our sweet neighbours have delivered two bagels, smoked salmon, gouda cheese, a grapefruit, and some marble cake—a Sunday treat! As I hear the feet departing down the corridor, I shout: "Thank you, Sandy!"

The Calm Before the Slip

LEA BEDDIA

. . . .

My daughter wakes at 3 am, the third time this week, calling out for her grandparents. I rock her back to sleep, but she's up again at five. I'm used to sleepless nights, but my daughter is too young to understand why we can't see loved ones, and her anxiety wakes us up.

As for the rest of the morning: cartoons, losing Monopoly to my boys, homeschooling, and a walk in the woods to keep us fit and busy.

This strange quiet is like the moment before slipping on the top step. It's calm, but I'm about to fall into my own anxiety. I distract myself and read to my kids atop heaps of toys, then clean up, only to have another mess erupt minutes later. These activities help me block out anything stressful, like waiting at home while my husband goes on a supply run. I'm worried school won't resume, I haven't seen my family in over a month, and I feel my heart break with every news broadcast.

It hits me all at once, and I have an urgent need to be alone. I take a moment to cry—not for myself, but for this broken world. I shift from overwhelmed to frustrated, and settle at helpless. I'm most concerned about my parents, who are in Montreal, locked away from my region in the north of Lanaudière, which these days feels like a distant planet. I worry for my students, without school as their safe constant, where they get free snacks and breakfast. To my surprise, I miss them immensely.

It's hard to explain, because I spend many working hours asking them to quiet down, but now, even though I'm busy, it's too quiet without them. I worry about the safety and health of those with difficult and unstable family situations, not just the threat of COVID-19. But I block it all out, so I can function.

I video chat with my parents, and watch my seventy-nine-year-old dad dance with my daughter. It's true love across internet connections, Wi-Fi, and a pandemic.

Later in the day, my husband and I pack up our kids and drive to his parents' house, only minutes away. We pile out, line up in front of our car, and belt out the least harmonious and most beautiful rendition of *Bonne fête, Mamie* across a driveway and into an open window. Before supper, we draw rainbows and leave thank-you notes in the mailbox for our mail carrier, who delivered books we ordered to keep us busy. We check on an elderly couple in town to see if they need supplies. We ease our worries with kindness for others and gratitude, because what else can we do? We enjoy our kids because, although I'd give it up in an instant to heal our world, I've been aching for extra time with them. And I'll rock my daughter to sleep again at 3 am tomorrow morning.

Learning to Share Boxes

JENNIFER DELESKIE

· · · · · ● · · · ·

I don't know how many stairs there are between The Boulevard and Summit Crescent, even though I've climbed them a dozen times over the past two weeks. If I did, I believe these stairs would feel more rooted in my world, like a poem committed to memory. I'm not present enough these days to count stairs or memorize poetry. I used to run on the Mountain, but now I stick to my neighbourhood, which is less familiar to me than I thought. Today, I saw Frère André's chapel for the first time. I watched a woman sweep her postage-stamp front lawn, making a small and meticulous pile of last year's leaves.

We received a large package a few days ago, and Theo, my thirteen-year-old, claimed the box. He's spending his days inside it, occasionally sharing the space with the cat, who is also fond of boxes. This strikes me as an odd impulse, but Theo has always sought out small places. When I last checked on him, he was eating salt and vinegar chips, and doing something on his phone.

My husband and I awoke at 4 am. We held hands for a while and then, once he was back asleep, I went to the guest room to read. The heroine of *Jamaica Inn* frustrates me. Why does she stay in that derelict inn with her horrible uncle? What prevents her from leaving?

My husband works in ER. I spend the day waiting for him to call, even though I'm sure he won't. If he touches his phone at work, he might contaminate it. I try to write, but my thoughts fail to solidify. I'm researching something called auxetics for my novel. When auxetic materials are stretched, they thicken rather than attenuate.

I wonder if there are substances that can expand and contract at the same time. I feel like this is what's happening to me.

At home again, my husband tells me that one of his favourite nurses lost it. Everyone in the emergency department is waiting for the storm. Some people find waiting easier than others.

Lillian, my eighteen-year-old, lounges on her bed downstairs reading *War with the Newts,* and I sit in front of my computer, opening tabs at random. A friend in Madrid has emailed to tell me that her father just died from COVID-19. She says the situation there is desperate, and she doesn't know how she's going to feed her family. Annabel, my sixteen-year-old, thumps around in the room beside me. I think she's doing an online workout with some friends.

We watch the final two episodes of *Tiger King,* all five of us on the king-size bed, and then the kids drift off to their rooms or their box. Tomorrow, my husband will return to the hospital to wait for the storm, and the rest of us will resume our existences inside the house, coming together and floating apart. But now it's time for sleep, or for whatever each of us does in the small hours of the night.

Waiting for the Apocalypse

SUREHKA SURENDRAN

. . . .

As an ER nurse, every day I wake up asking myself what my day will be like. Will it be relaxing? In what section will I work? Will any of my patients end up being intubated? When is the apocalypse coming to the hospital?

Every morning is pretty much the same. At 10 am, I get out of bed and make myself breakfast. I eat while watching a series on Netflix. By 1 pm, I put on the news to watch the Quebec press conference.

There's no such thing as a typical day in the ER. We might see similar scenarios, but each person is different. Our ER is experiencing fewer incoming patients, but higher acuity—which means more people who are actually sick. Before the pandemic, many people came in with less severe complaints. But now, real emergencies mix with some cases that COVID-19 protocols rule out. So, without these less acute complaints, the flow for the typical ER nurse has changed. It's quieter than I have ever seen it! It feels like an eerie calm before the storm. I'm trying to prepare mentally for what the coming weeks and months will hold.

I usually take public transport to go to work but, since the pandemic, my boyfriend takes me. I arrive around 3:45 pm. At the entrance, I show my employee card to the security guard, because we only want hospital workers to enter the building, not any family members or visitors. The security guard squirts disinfectant into my hands, and off I go to change into my scrubs. Thereafter, my colleagues and I wait for our assignments to see to which section of the ER we'll be assigned. At 3:59 pm, we get up, and before going to our designated section, we go and get our rare and precious procedure mask. I say "rare" and "precious," because there aren't many masks left.

We used to have masks lying around everywhere but, when the pandemic started, many masks were stolen and therefore our assistant head nurse is controlling their distribution. Since we are facing community transmission of the virus, every healthcare worker must wear a procedure mask at all times. I think connecting through facial expressions is an important part of being human. It's one of the ways that, as a nurse, I show reassurance and empathy. It's hard to show emotion behind a mask and eye protector, but now it's even more important. I try to express care by being a grounded presence and a calm spirit, and by listening.

The ER floor has changed. Most of the rooms have been covered in plastic, to become the COVID rooms. It almost looks like a construction site. Doctors, nurses, and beneficiary attendants are dressed with protective eyewear, masks, and scrub caps. I walk through the field to give the best care that I possibly can. Entering a room with a patient who is COVID + is a weird feeling. It's familiar because, as a nurse, I have taken care of patients a million times, but the threat and paranoia of a silent killer is very much present in the room. I become much more cognizant of every move I make. I am always disinfecting or washing my hands before and after every move. My hands have never been so damaged. Reusing the same mask over and over again. Constantly adjusting to new rules as we get to know more about the virus. Everyday the rules change, and it's hard to keep track. I have to think about everything I need before entering a COVID room, or I'll be singing like Adele, "Hello from the other side... in need of help!"

If a patient deteriorates, I stay in the room for at least an hour or more with the proper PPE, while a colleague on the other side prepares what the doctor prescribed. It's called teamwork. We charge into chaos when any other sane person would be running away. When you come out of these rooms sweating and take off your N-95 mask, it leaves a mark like a small bruise. Sometimes it feels like we're fighting a forest fire with squirt guns.

At 11:59 pm, I give my report to the night nurse. I get out of my scrubs and put on my clothes. I wave goodbye to colleagues and say goodnight. As I walk by the entrance where the security guard will give me disinfectant, I see my boyfriend waiting in his car. I tell him about my shift. I can see in his eyes that he is shocked about what he's hearing; at the same time, he is proud of me and of the hard work I'm doing.

A Day in the Life...

LOUISE CARSON

. . . .

8:20 am. Large male ginger cat scratches at bedroom door. Snuffles.
8:21 am. Piercing yowls from small black female cat.

8:22 am. Sigh. Rise. Assess back stiffness, pain. Open door. Greet cats. Shuffle to bathroom. Ablutions. Cat-box duty. Cats jostle for position waiting to use clean box. Feed them.

8:35 am. Feed husky. Take her out for pee. Coffee. Write, sitting on sofa under two cats. Best part of day.

10 am. Dress. Walk dog. Rain. Good. Privacy of personal gloom ensured. Pick up dog poop.

10:30 am. Dry off dog. Prevent cats from escaping from house. Take cats out one by one in my arms to experience rain. They don't like it. Second coffee. Second go at cat box.

10:45 am. Check emails and literary administrative tasks. Cats still want to go out. Yowl and bat at the keys in back-door lock. Try to ignore them. Write some more.

12 pm. Make lunch and eat while listening to feds. (Ignored Justin at 11 am again. Sorry, Justin.)

1 pm. Tea with Premier Legault. Not a fan of Dr. Arruda. Prefer soft anxious B.C. chief doctor. Back feels better.

1:30 pm. Walk dog again, but in the other direction. Rain. Good. Soft drops on my face. Pick up poop.

2 pm. Dry off dog. Prevent cats from escaping. Tell them it's raining. They ignore me. Type what I wrote. Revise. Research. E-mail. Cats fight each other all over the house.

3 pm. Phone a friend. He's 79. His daughter leaves his food at the end of his driveway. He's resigned to dying anyway, he says. His bad heart. We laugh. Water my plants while we are talking. Cats sleeping.

4 pm. Watch a nine-year-old episode of *Escape to the Country*. They are in Devon. They are always in Devon. Realize I have escaped to the country. Cat box during the commercials.

5 pm. Feed pets. Think about supper. Watch news instead. Do Sudoku.

6 pm. Still thinking, watching, doing. Open a can. Make toast. What's for dessert?

7 pm. Walk dog. Misty. Good. Mild. Bloody winter's done.

7:30 pm. Dry dog's feet. Very dirty on the road. Look at the day's dishes. Not too many. Leave them for tomorrow and make tea. Wipe kitchen counter.

8 pm. Watch whatever British drama is on Vision TV. Tonight it's *Doc Martin*. He and Louisa seem to be working it out. I wonder about their sex life. Cats vie for lap. Dog on sofa next to me.

9 pm. *The National*. Many dead everywhere. Also many alive. Cat box and brush teeth during commercials.

10 pm. Read e-mails. Turn off computer. Get into bed and read one of Mankell's, preferably a Wallender. Cats snuggle. Second-best part of day. Fall asleep.

Midnight. Wake up and take dog out for last pee. The sky has cleared. I look up at the stars.

The Self-Isolation Playlist

MARK FOSS

· · · · · · · ·

I am in a fallow period with my writing, awaiting one of several ideas to take hold, unwilling to force-feed my imagination. So when *I wake* in early morning, I don't rush to the computer. I lie flat in the dark, but I get restless after a few minutes. How do I rub sleep from my eyes without touching my face?

I reach for my phone to check mail and Facebook notifications. I belong to a group in which people post music related in some way to our collective moment. Yesterday, the host posted a self-isolation playlist of Beatles' songs with transformed titles, such as "I Don't Want to Hold Your Hand." I invented a few titles, got some new likes and loves overnight, but not enough. Why is it never enough?

I walk down the sombre hall to open a door that will let in a little light through the tiny rectangle that passes as a front-door window. I open the blind in my office and then turn on the computer, feeling tightness in my chest. What if it doesn't start up?

I live alone and work from home, so self-isolation is my normal life on steroids. When the crisis took hold in Italy, I lost paid writing work immediately: I have a client in Rome. Another editing contract was postponed a month. What other words might have come that didn't or won't?

I am grateful to have enough work. So many friends in the film or service industries will be applying for relief on Monday. But the benefits of work go beyond money. Without work, or a novel to write, how long before I start climbing the walls? Dangerous, because the walls are covered with my literary heroes, and there is no getting past them. When someone quotes Fernando Pessoa on Facebook,

I resist the impulse to comment with a postcard from my shrine. Instead, I post The Moody Blues' "The Best Way to Travel" on the music group page, which echoes the Pessoa quotation: "One need only exist to travel." What is this incessant need to make connections that no one else sees?

Apart from trying to elicit likes, loves, and laughs from strangers, I write an acquaintance who works in long-term care and talk twice to an old friend in Ottawa. I am too driven today to stop for my twenty minutes of YouTube yoga, or to break for Franz Kafka's *Diaries* in mid-afternoon. Nor do I walk through the park, because it's grey and autumn-like, a disappointment after the spring-like Saturday. So why, after four hours of listening to Bill Evans on Spotify, do I switch to Autumn's "Grey Solace"?

After six hours of editing a policy document, and two hours of writing a first draft of this diary, I settle down with leftovers to binge on *Money Heist* on Netflix. I am tired of questions.

Watching Time Melt

MARIANNE ACKERMAN

· · · · · · · ·

8 am. I wake up to the smell of coffee, my husband bearing a tray with cereal, yogurt, blueberries. The bundle of newspapers he tosses on the bed is huge, so I know it's Saturday. We read silently, the best bits out loud. Grim news, yet there is solace to be found in knowing, in digesting thoughts developed by smart people who are paying attention.

The oddest thing about quarantine is how little it has changed the rhythm of my normal day. In one respect my life is better: My normal writerly anxieties about productivity and purpose are shared by millions. Nobody has railed against the canny time-sponge of Facebook more than I, but today it's a vital forum brimming with information, insight, wicked humour, meltdowns. I force myself to stop, shift the laptop to a small side table, leaving the larger one free and clean, inviting ideas. I actually get out a fountain pen.

In a flash, it's lunchtime. Over soup, my officemate/husband and I catch up on events. Time feels like Salvador Dali's melting watch painting. Every writer's life is a battle with time. If you sense time passing, you are not writing. Not good. The greatest joy comes after writing. But I promised my grandson we'd make cookies, so line up at PA for an hour to get ingredients, plus as much fresh produce as I can carry home.

3:30 pm. Reach eleven-year-old Oskar on Hangouts. He's in bed with a blanket over his face, insists he's in the kitchen. Pranking is his thing. By the time he finds a mixing bowl, I realize I'd rather watch him smash around than make cookies myself. The result is an interactive home movie of my daughter and our boy arguing their way through Martha Stewart's "nutritious" oatmeal cookies. Only two substitutions, tastings at every step. Ten bite-sized cookies make it into the oven. How many per family member? "Three, and one extra for me," he says. Check math lesson.

4:30 pm. Zoom conference with two actors in Belleville, Ontario. We're rehearsing a scene from my soon-to-be published book *Triplex Nervosa Trilogy* for possible online broadcast. They're great. Whew! I'd secretly feared the play could only work with its original Montreal cast. But what about atmosphere? Chemistry? They're in separate rooms, under fierce lighting. This feels like work. Work is great. Next rehearsal is set for Monday 8 pm, when it will be dark outside. Natural atmosphere.

6 pm. Time for the Trump show. How far can he go? Comedy and fear are an unlikely combination, yet appropriate to our times. One of my favourite series is HBO's *Barry*, about a hired killer who is also trying to break into acting. Delicious absurdity, the clash of worlds finds pathos in both. Unusual juxtapositions are my thing these days.

7 pm. Dinner includes fresh asparagus. I think of the truck drivers hauling them here from Mexico or California. So many sleepless hours. Truck stops are closed en route, forcing them to pee in ditches, for the sake of our supper. We lift our glasses in gratitude.

The New Line Dance

AMI SANDS BRODOFF

. . . .

Today is my eldest son Tobias' twenty-seventh birthday. He is in New York, and I am here in Montreal. The distance has never felt so vast.

I'm on my usual five-kilometre walk from my home in western NDG to the top of Monkland Village and then back. I text Toby birthday wishes and love. I'm worried about him.

It's the first beautiful early spring day with a clear blue sky and streams of buttery sun that feel almost warm, the snow nearly melted but for patches revealing moist gouges of earth and sodden brown leaves. There are mothers shepherding kids on bicycles and scooters, dog walkers, and folks just getting a breath of air. I do the new line dance, shuffle-slide-step-left, shuffle-slide-step-right, to maintain a two-metre distance from my fellow humans. Pandemic platitudes echo through my mind: *We are all in this together! We are further apart but closer together!* I sense the look on my face is not simpatico—more like a grimace or glare. I'm not used to this extra layer of consciousness of keeping my distance, of viewing my neighbours as threats, potential carriers of a deadly virus.

In pre-pandemic days, one of my pleasures was running into friends and acquaintances and stopping to hug and chat. I don't meet anyone today. Another is buying our family's favourite porridge bread at *La Meunerie Urbaine*. I see they're open, but I'm skittish about venturing inside. I walk on past Zone—good, old Zone!— where I might find the need for some pool-blue ceramic mugs, or a set of bamboo place mats for entertaining. Ah entertaining!

As I walk, I think of my new coping strategies: limit news (while obsessively immersing myself in it), write (while feeling anxious and distracted), check in with friends and family (though I find Zoom weird and alienating). I've promised myself to get a bit of exercise and fresh air each day. I need those endorphins and moving helps with anxiety.

Tobias is a third-year medical student in New York City, epicentre of the COVID-19 crisis. As I write, one person dies every two-and-a-half minutes from the virus, bringing the death toll over 3,000, a gale-force crisis in which more than 102,000 people have tested positive. Tobias goes into the hospital most days, as Governor Cuomo has enlisted medical students: all hands needed on deck. Toby and I will talk later. I long to hear his voice.

I'm fortunate to have my husband, Michael, and my younger son, Gabriel, in my quarantine pod at home. Ordinarily, I would hardly see Gabriel, as he is so busy with university and friends, but now, we share most meals and discuss poetry. This morning, it was *A Sand Book,* by Ariana Reines.

As I pass the shuttered Melk Café, I think about how I miss crowds and hubbub, which is the opposite of how I feel normally. I imagine waiting in line at Melk, amid the din, ordering my latte and apple cinnamon scone, finding there is no place to sit. Then I spot Toby, books sprawled out. He glances up, sees me, and motions me over to share his tiny table. I squish in, elated and relieved.

Postscript: *Tobias became infected with COVID-19 in July, about three months after this post, as did many of his medical school peers. He has recovered and returned to the hospital for work, as the pandemic rages on.*

Normal Circumstances

MICHELLE ARISS

· · · · · · · · ·

Normal Circumstances.
Saturday, April 4, 2020: the fourth day of the fourth month of a leap year, the spring most of us wish we could just leap over. Go directly to summer or even further, into autumn, instead of pandemic "jail," although the quarters to which I am confined are about as far from a prisoner's four walls as they can be. So, no complaints here, unless I talk about the fact that, at the age of seventy, I moved from the Eastern Townships, where I had lived for close to two decades, to a neighbouring bilingual city in Ontario, where I know no one. The closest family member lives a good hour away by car.

Not because I had family or friends here in my city of choice. I wanted to make a new start after the end of a relationship, to reconnect with my native province. I left behind wonderful friends in Quebec, both francophone and anglophone, who, I believed and still believe, will always be my friends. Under normal circumstances, the city where I live makes it easy for me to visit them, and vice-versa. I'm outgoing, I told myself, and, under normal circumstances, it shouldn't take me long to meet people. I love playing tennis, and there are two courts directly across from my new house. Tennis is a good way to get to know people, right? Under normal circum-stances—yes, it is.

Under normal circumstances, the city I moved to offers a variety of cultural attractions. In one of several past lives, I've lived in other provinces, even another country. Long before I moved to Quebec, live theatre brought challenges and friendships into my life. This new city, I knew, had two vibrant theatre companies. They would rekindle the embers of that interest, I assured myself. Discovering the history and beauty of nearby towns and villages while cycling the area's country roads would keep me healthy, and enrich my attitude toward this new beginning. Moreover, I have no grown-up children cautioning me otherwise out of concern for my well-being. What is stopping me, I asked? I knew I was up to the challenge. I had done the research. I made the decision.

Now, on this sunny Saturday, I question that decision. Under normal circumstances, I would not do that. "Never look back," advised a sometimes-wise former husband. However, as my dear friends tell me of their grandchildren greeting them through the front window, of their neighbours leaving baked goods and "stay safe" cards outside the door for them, I do look back on the choice I made (was it really only six months ago?). Grateful every day for my good health, for efficient governments and generous essential workers, and for technology that in my youth was the stuff of science-fiction, still, I ask myself, "if I had known the world would come to this, would I be here, alone in this new city, longing for the return of normal circumstances?"

Days of Guilt

CAROLINE VU

· · · · · · · ·

I know I did nothing wrong. I did not travel. I did not party. I did not cough in anyone's face. Yet I feel guilty. I look downward on my way to the grocery store. I wear dark glasses to mask my Asian features. I smile apologetically at the woman on the bus as she shoos me away. By accident, my sanitized fingers had touched her rubber-gloved hands. Her reaction surprises me. I didn't realize it was such a big deal. The accidental grazing of two hands—I didn't know it was the new social sin.

The woman's pouting mouth worries me. Her "hmmmpphhh!" brings back memories of my childhood in Connecticut. 1971. I was 11. The Vietnam War was at its peak. American GIs were coming back in body bags. I saw all that on television. I tried to hide, but accusing looks followed me everywhere. Being the only Vietnamese family in town, we were an easy target. "Why is your father not fighting your own war?" people wanted to know. "Why do my sons need to die for you guys?" they asked. Having no answer, I kept quiet. My mother and I, we learned to smile and bow respectfully. Guilt-ridden, we could only mutter: "Sorry, sir!" My father was still in Vietnam, too old to fight. I knew it, yet didn't say so. Protesting wouldn't change anything. We were already guilty.

"Oh, get over it! The Vietnam War is long finished. Those Connecticut days are done with!" my daughter exclaims. As a biracial child born in Canada, she feels completely at home in North America. She sees her heritage as a bonus. Hers is a generation of open-minded, multi-cultural kids. She'd never think she'd be singled out until she hears, "Chinese go home!" one day. Turning around, she sees nobody.

Korean men beaten on the streets. Bricks thrown at Chinese restaurants. Vietnamese pagodas destroyed. A president insisting on the term, "China Virus." The newspapers are full of such stories. I should be angry. Instead, I feel guilty. I feel guilty for not speaking up. I feel guilty for not doing the right thing. All these years in Canada, taking advantage of the country's generosity, of its free healthcare and affordable education, what did I give in return, aside from paying my taxes? What did I do with my time, aside from prescribing birth-control pills, treating ear infections, fixing bedsores, and filling insurance claims? The free-flowing water, the unrestricted soap, the unlimited access to masks, the large space to isolate myself socially—do I merit it? I think of relatives in Vietnam stuck in cramped apartments; I think of Montreal's homeless persons unable to wash their hands; I think of writer friends struggling to pay the rent; I think of sleepless medical colleagues on the front line—and the guilt surges. I tell myself things will change. Tomorrow, I'll sign up for one of those COVID-19 clinics. I'll control the guilt.

PENNING THE PANDEMIC
A Body Divided

JOE BONGIORNO

. . . .

I jog on the gravel path by the train tracks. I readjust my surgical mask and stray onto the grass to maintain a two-metre distance from a cyclist. My butt throbs. Pain gives way to numbness. Hamstring nerves are pinched. I'm out of breath. My lungs open up to the cool air; I am fortunate to be left breathless by exercise and not COVID-19.

I had spent the past three years in my own quarantine-of-sorts, sequestered in the near isolation of my office, hunched over a laptop. I had typed feverishly to complete a novel by a looming, yet self-imposed deadline, and on the very day that I typed the last words of my manuscript—a novel about a future pandemic—my city, country, and the world at large, shut down.

The novel was complete, but my confinement was extended indefinitely. I wilted. While churning out words at night, I had slogged through the corrections of my students' assignments during the day. My body had become idle and flabby. I had cut myself off from sensory experience. Going for a walk, attending family dinners, and conversing with friends were all detours from my goal. Everything was an obstacle to completing the manuscript. *Everything.* There was wine in my glass and food on my plate, but I wasn't really tasting them. I finally noticed my person being divided in two, as the distance between body and mind grew further apart. My head might as well have separated from my body at the neck.

Can a commitment to making art ever be detrimental? How can trying to craft a beautiful or meaningful thing be anything but fulfilling? Plenty of films tell the story of a writer or painter, aspiring or established, enraptured and then swallowed by the object of creation. You know the trope: the tortured artist. You have to suffer for your art, it is said. But does this devotion, if not tempered, stifle the artist's productivity? Even a machine wears down, if not properly maintained.

Shakespeare wrote *King Lear* while in lockdown from the Black Death. Frankly, I don't care how productive old William was back in his day. I have little desire to write at the moment, and, for the first time in as long as I can remember, I don't mind not caring. The *Top Ten Ways to Be a Productive Writer* have vanished from my mind.

Despite the manifold tragedies this virus has unleashed, and despite the isolation of confinement, I have experienced a paradoxical freedom. Normalcy has been fragmented, interrupted for the foreseeable future, so why shouldn't I seize upon the opportunity to approach writing differently? Not hit the brakes, but rather slow down and be more *active* in the experience of capturing the world as I see it, instead of idly observing from the distance of my office desk.

At a time when bodies are being destroyed by a new virus, I am slowly getting in touch with my own. Each step forward on the gravel path serves to reattach my head—so often caught up in the imaginings of a new story—to its place on my shoulders. What I want is to take the world in: the sidewalk lined with irrepressible dandelions, the graffitied brick walls of the neighbourhood, and the gusts of wind carrying the compost stink of summer.

My thoughts return to the jog, to being in my body, the physical me experiencing the stones under foot and the sweat dripping into my eyes. My *King Lear* can wait. I will get around to it when I am ready, but, for now, I return to the rhythm of my own breath.

Home Alone

CONSTANTIN POLYCHRONAKOS

• • • • • • • • •

C all it an opportunity to catch up with all the things I have been postponing. Call it an opportunity to meditate on the illusion of certainty. But what am I doing today, cocooning all alone in the safety of my apartment, phoning, e-mailing, and Zooming with my non-urgent patients? Is singing *So Long, Marianne* out the window the best I can do? I should have been on the front lines, in the emergency room, in the intensive care, fighting COVID-19 in a hail of droplets. I know I am invincible! I know I can beat the coronavirus—I have already vanquished it, caught it by the horns, and wrestled it to the ground, with only a few bruises to show for it.

Rewind back to the twenty-fifth of November, when Corona was still only something you were served in a bar. (Remember?) The public transit fanatic that I am, I took several rides packed like a sardine in the Beijing subway system, then dined in a restaurant so crowded that my Chinese colleague and I had to share our table with total strangers. One has to travel to East Asia to appreciate what "crowded" means. I spent the last night at an airport hotel packed with travellers, half of whom were from Wuhan (or so it feels), before flying back to Montreal. Ten days later, still three weeks before the first worrisome news from China, I came down with the worst (by far) respiratory infection of my adult life. Two days in bed, not taking antipyretics, concentrating on how the same cytokines that gave me high fever, aches, and pains and made me almost too weak to get out of bed, were the ones that were demolishing the virus. No cough medicine, either, of course! How foolish to suppress the most powerful mechanism our body has for clearing respiratory infections.

In forty-eight hours, I was out of bed and feeling almost back to normal, although some coughing continued for a couple of weeks. Still coughing, I flew to Vancouver, to spend the holidays with my daughter and two-year-old granddaughter both of whom, within days, had the same symptoms—but much milder and for a shorter period. The kid had a fever for only an evening, and was back to her usual bundle of joy and energy the following morning.

By the time we heard that COVID-19 had probably been kicking around in China since October, it was too late to get myself tested for the virus. Antibodies last much longer, so I will get the blood test as soon as I can do it without bumping off someone else who needs it more urgently. I need to know. Perhaps I *am* invincible! Perhaps I can donate the antibodies in my blood to save a life. Perhaps I can be reassigned to the front line. At the very least, I am a serious contender for The First Canadian Case.

Fear

IAN THOMAS SHAW

· · · · ● · · ● ·

I walk toward the entrance, mustering the courage to put on the mask. I pull it out, adjust it as I have seen it done on Youtube, and jam my hands back into my pockets. A guard approaches. He stops six feet away and says: "*Vos mains.*" I start to raise my hands into the air, when he nods toward a portable sink in the corner. Dutifully, I shuffle over to it. The water is lukewarm, the liquid soap cheap and slimy. "*Vingt secondes!*" I nod at this new command.

A young girl sprays sanitizer on the shopping cart's handle. She rubs it vigorously. With a smile, the enthusiasm of youth, she signals it's good to go. I shake my head and motion to a larger cart. She grits her teeth at my lack of appreciation, and begins to spray and rub a bigger one.

The first aisle is empty. I eye the produce, wondering how many infected paws have judged its freshness that day. Canned veggies and fruit will do instead. The fresh steaks entice me. The butcher rubs his nose with the back of his hand. Canned tuna will be fine. A lone woman approaches me from the dairy section. I adjust my mask. She turns into the canned soup aisle. The soup can wait.

Toilet paper has mercifully returned to its rightful place. Gone are the empty shelves of the previous week. I grab a twelve-pack, then decide to go for the jumbo pack instead. The soup lady is at the cashier's. She glares at me when I put back the twelve-pack and reach for the larger one. I realize I've forgotten my gloves. I pull them out and wave them at her. But the damage is done. She whispers something to the cashier who shakes her head. I put on the gloves, grab my precious booty, turn, and march down the aisle. Their eyes drill into my back.

The other shoppers disperse at the sight of my mask. I want to shout: "Look, this mask is for you! To protect you, not me!" I feel like Bernie Sanders urging the crowd: "Not me. Us!" But that didn't work out for him either, did it?

The cashier sizes me up through a thick sheet of Plexiglas. My cart is overflowing with canned food, pasta, hand sanitizer, and the jumbo pack. She whispers, as if not to anger me: "*Deux bouteilles par client.*" I nod as she gingerly sets aside the extra bottles of Purell. When I tap my credit card to pay, it's beyond my tap limit, so I push it in the machine, and clumsily punch in my code with my gloved hands. As I put the bags into the cart, the cashier opens the confiscated sanitizer and douses the keypad. I bite my lip and think of how people have been brainwashed into fearing the mask. I fear the unmasked.

Taking Flight While Staying Put

BABSIE CHALIFOUX-REIS

. . . .

My days have been spent in fear. Not in fear of getting sick, but of a myriad of other factors I didn't know I needed to fear. At first, my anxieties were practical in nature. I feared losing my job, which I did, and losing my apartment, which I didn't. Then came the restlessness.

Having resigned myself to the circumstances, I, like many others, found myself housebound. As a flight attendant for most of my adult life, my world has shrunk dramatically. Home has always been a place I have cherished, because my return has always been fleeting. After nearly a month of confinement, it dawns on me that I've never gone this long without boarding an airplane. Part of me believes that I needed this. I try to see it as an opportunity to become more appreciative of the things and people I've taken for granted. However, it's become increasingly difficult to appreciate anything when the simple act of walking out the front door elicits suspicion.

I find it absurd that, in the world we now find ourselves, two brothers living under the same roof would be considered a threat if they chose to go outside and kick a ball around. It seems petty that we should deny them that freedom, simply because it is also denied to those of us who live alone. And, although I can see the complications in monitoring those kinds of activities and I understand the need for precaution, it's terrifying how willing we are to relinquish our freedoms when confronted with our most basic fears.

Most sinister of all, however, is our continued insistence on demonizing the other. Present-day targets are all those who still refuse to fall in line. We've essentially begun to police each other, neighbour spying on neighbour, alerting the authorities to anything unusual. People have turned to social media as a means to further alienate and shame society's menaces. We are so quick to judge and condemn strangers, when all we know about them is a single action they might've committed, usually taken out of context. Our communal fear has turned us into something that I'm personally more afraid of than this virus. We're creating a society that breeds paranoia and suspicion.

I can see how this pandemic has the potential to bring out the worst in people, but I also know that there's much potential for good. This threat has the power to unite those who would otherwise have nothing else in common. I often worry about what life will look like on the other side of this disaster. I worry about the economy, obviously, and about how people are going to make ends meet, but mostly I worry about our collective consciousness. My hope is that we won't let fear get the best of us, so that we can still recognize ourselves when the shock wears off.

The Day Full of Minutes

MARY THALER

· · · · · ● · · · ·

20 *March*
A bad day is when
In the minutes after waking
In the minutes that come after the waking minutes
When you're awake, and you see all the minutes that are coming
A day full of minutes, a river of sand
Each one a parched universe
Fluttering wisps of appointments, lists, and poor decisions
And all of them empty

22 March
Mr. Crow, you could be anywhere in the world
Dusty-hooded among the temple pillars or
Wide-winging over echoing ice. You could be
Feasting with dead famous people,
Or finding cursed relics
Or giving your opinion on the nightly news
But for twelve years, you've brought your lunch outside my window
To this eavestrough of twigs and tiny bones
And eaten it

24 March
By order, time's mutation shall be marked,
Not by this wild and rampant spring
But with a menu grid
A grocery list, thoughtfully composed
A comfort that doesn't let me down.

Don't call me, unless it's to ask whether all tablespoons are really equal
Or if you can truly know the moisture content of your flour
From now on, I will read only cookbooks
Flicking through pages quicker than they can do me good
Absorbing this warning:
Results may vary.

29 March
This may surprise you but
Instead of the walls, it's me that's shrinking
In my leaky apartment, with its cells of warm and cool
I fall more and more into a smudge, a scale
A snag, chip, scrap, loose thread.
A moth got inside while I brought in my mail
And buzzes nightly at the top of my window
He doesn't understand.
It's such a small thing he wants
To change this loud abyss for sky
And be enfolded by the night

3 April
It's never more than clarity's illusion
The body rousing with purposes the mind still gropes after
The ravens echo over asphalt frost
And the sun leans out in wild surmise
There is all the time in the world, and the world is
A hoop circling down-slope to forever
With a warm hum, fingers alight on the keyboard
Ready to make words.
But time, accumulating in staticky drifts
Flounders forward through spiny growth
The joggers and delivery trucks appear
While I stare for ten minutes at a single headline
Then look down to see the last of my vision
Sedimented at the bottom of a mug

Days Without Agenda

BERNICE ANGELINE SORGE

· · · · · · · ·

M y agenda was a small book I carried everywhere. I used to fill
it up with dates and times of when and where I had to be.
It guided my days and projected my life weeks into the future. Since
the COVID-19 isolation, my agenda is no longer a book; it is a
fluid movement from place to place and project to project on my
seven-acre homestead, where I have lived for over forty years. Inside
the house, I paint, draw, and write—things I would usually do at
my spacious church studio. An early spring this year has helped to
inspire me to work outside on the land, to design a huge vegetable
garden, contrary to my original plans to make the garden smaller
this year. It all depends on the weather and the changing situation
of the pandemic.

This morning when I woke up, it was twelve degrees. I felt like
working outside. I would continue with the project I started a few
days earlier of digging up small tree stumps on a piece of land near
the house. I had decided to increase the size of the potato garden.
Donning my rubber boots, sun hat, and work gloves, and, of course,
with my phone and eyeglasses in my pockets, I grabbed shovels, saw,
axe, and clippers, opened the door and—lo and behold!—the frogs
were back early.

I dropped my tools, readied my phone for some video and,
instead of gardening, I made my way down to the pond. The surface
was scattered with these googly-eyed, noisy tourists floating with
legs spread out, letting the breeze and the water take them where
they may. It seemed like a wild celebration of liberation. I stood by
the pond for a long time. I found I could orchestrate the sounds

of the frogs either by being very still and letting them croak or by moving one arm up to lean on a birch trunk to silence all the voices. The croaks returned gradually, as I stood like a statue—a few tenors here, a few baritones there, to a final crescendo of voices all at once. Where was I?

Oh yes, the tree trunks! The reason I went outside this morning! I took some shots, put my phone back in my pocket and gathered up my discarded tools. I shovelled, pulled, cut, clipped, and sawed branches, pieces of buried wire, and roots. I worked until my joints and muscles started to ache.

Just in time to get inside and hear Premier Legault's daily conference on the virus. I listened and had flashes of what was going on out there, where I am not supposed to go. It's been almost four weeks confined to this wild little paradise with erratic internet connection.

Tomorrow, my muscles will feel sore from digging. Maybe I will take a break and write some poetry, or take time to get past the title on that novel I started twenty years ago. Maybe!

I'll start the day with what there is.

Of Magnolias During the End Times

JILL GOLDBERG

· · · · · · · · ·

6:30 am: Amelia the flying cat wakes me up. She's figured out that jumping on my head is a good way to get fed, while jumping on my husband's head is a good way to get herself flung out of the bedroom.

8:30 am: Wake in earnest. The sun is out, as it has been since isolation began. This is good, because isolation in Vancouver in January would feel even more apocalyptic. To be honest, it's been pretty hard to get in the pandemic mood when the magnolias are blossoming. Don't they know these are end times? Who dressed this set?

8:45 am: Set intentions for the day: work on novel, get over coronavirus + economic slowdown-induced gloom in order to work up courage to email agent; set schedule for handwashing.

9 am: Coffee. Read news excessively.

9:30 am: Where have all my students gone? Three weeks ago, when we went online, I needed a weedwhacker to get through the dozens of anxiety-ridden emails. Now my inbox is a silent wilderness. This is worrying, because my creative non-fiction students are supposed to submit their memoirs soon, and most of them haven't sent a first draft. Now is exactly when they need to be observing, writing, reflecting, but I'm guessing that, like me, they're watching *Tiger King* and making home videos of their cats. How has my brain gotten so squirrelly, so quickly? And, seriously, where are my students? At first, we had such a sense of solidarity in burrowing through this strange time, but now I'm the only one still talking.

11 am: Husband slips out to smoke a cigarette. We both pretend he's going for a walk. When he comes back, he picks up the cat for

a cuddle. I pick her up next. Feeling especially witty, I sniff her fur and announce: "I think Amelia's taken up smoking again." Sustained silent glaring ensues. I self-isolate in the bedroom office.

1 pm: Zoom meeting. Same as last week's meeting, but with more unruly hair, plus last week I was wearing pants. Touch my face one hundred times during meeting.

2-7 pm: Cook and eat and wash the dishes. Mark five essays. Read the news. Repeat.

7:30 pm: My husband has been on the phone and FaceTime for thirty minutes with my parents, explaining how to use Zoom in time for our Passover seder. He's a total gem, but I still manage to find daily opportunities to stir up conflict or berate him arbitrarily.

10 pm: If, during the day, I manage to forget, the nightly news broadcast reminds me: Thousands, tens of thousands, hundreds of thousands are sick, dying, gone. Today, the virus silenced John Prine. Who will be next? And who will be left to grieve? And what world will remain for those who survive?

I fall into sleep, anxious to escape the tedium and numb the terror. I am one of the lucky ones who will wake tomorrow with a cat on my head and blossoms—ephemeral, surreal, blessedly real—out my window.

Proud to Be a Boomer Zoomer

JOANNE GORMLEY

. . . .

On Wednesday morning, I wake to the sad news that John Prine has died from complications due to the coronavirus. He was seventy-three, just three years older than I am. My partner and I listen to him on YouTube singing *When I Get to Heaven... I'll shake God's hand, then I'll get me a cocktail... kiss a pretty girl on a tilt-a-whirl.* I hope he is.

Wanting to keep as much regularity in my days as I can, I retrieve the *Montreal Gazette* from my front porch. With a solution of water and bleach, I spray every section, front and back, and drape them over the backs of the kitchen chairs. While they dry, I lay out my yoga mat and teach my class via Zoom, rather proud to be a boomer Zoomer, as my grandsons call me. I have multiple views into the homes of people I've been missing. We wave and smile, then practise staying centred and calm in these disturbing times. At the end, we chant our usual OM, offering well-being for our families and friends and the frontline workers.

The new directive I read about in the paper rattles my equanimity. Masks might indeed be effective. We are being encouraged to wear them. Not having bought any, I stuff a cloth napkin into my jacket pocket, but once outside I can't bear to tie it over my mouth. I want to breathe easily. Am I being selfish? Am I a carrier?

I zigzag my way around the people on Queen Mary Road, past the nursing home where seven people have died, up the hill to St. Joseph's Oratory, and into the winding roads of upper Westmount to the summit. This daily walk is essential. The cardinals and robins, the cheery chirps of the sparrows hidden in the greening hedges are hopeful sounds of renewal. The other walkers and I share this sanctuary. We are subdued and quiet, acknowledging each other's presence with a small nod or a faint smile. We catch the sun on our faces and breathe in the spring breeze as we walk, distant but connected.

Back on Queen Mary, there is surprisingly no line up at the pharmacy. The masked clerk squirts a shot of sanitizer into my hands and then, without warning, picks up a white gun from the table and holds it to my forehead. Startled by this new security measure, for a moment I think I am about to join John Prine. I get the okay. My temperature is acceptable.

The gold foil-wrapped bunnies and coloured eggs look brightly festive on the shelves. I carefully select two of each for my grandsons for their Easter morning backyard hunt. I'll leave the treats on my daughter's porch and will have to imagine the kids' chocolate smeared faces and warm hugs. I'm too vulnerable, my daughter says, to be near them.

Back home, I prepare dinner, waiting for my partner to return from work. We'll listen to Prine tonight, while we play rummy, hoping to draw the luckiest cards we can.

Witches' Circles and Dragon Eyes

CAROLYNN RAFMAN

. . . .

Haibun. A boy.
My daughter parks in the empty lot. Wagging her tail, the big puppy leaps onto Thomas. He says laughingly: "Hi Nana Banana!" No hugging. No kissing cheeks. He hops onto his small bicycle, fastens his helmet, and speeds off to the water's edge, suited up in neoprene, immune to the drizzle.

Yesterday, the Verdun bike path teemed with families, strollers, dog walkers, stand-up paddle boarders, kayakers, frisbee players. Bare skin exposed to sun. Today, the mist comforts us. Fewer people are out walking, fewer bodies to keep at a distance. Pairs of honking geese drop into the current. A mallard takes flight into the wind. Listen: a solitary woodpecker.

Thomas transitions easily from the paved path through mud puddles into the wild brush skirting the river. We meet a busy robin redbreast. I point out trees felled by beaver teeth. He opens my umbrella like a shield, as we slip deeper into the gnarly woods rolling his small frame over a fallen tree that blocks our way. Are we in a witches' circle? He picks up the perfect stick and holds it high, a magic sword to poke the coals from ancient fires. Wearing boots with dragon eyes, he zigzags over pointy rocks and tree roots. "I've got this Nana!" he calls out confidently.

We reach the point where land ends, where the mighty St. Lawrence River widens under the Champlain Bridge. 12 pm Sunday. The bells of Notre Dame des Sept Douleurs begin to ring, synchronized throughout our city to lift the spirit. Closed retail stores offer workers a break, but none may enter church.

Thomas digs up smooth black stones and takes aim, determined and delighted to hear them splash in the calm water. The pup jumps up and down, but not in. The boy is not in any hurry to leave this location. Maybe a fisherman, *or woman,* he adds, will still come. Lunchtime. Back by the dog park, empty and locked, filled with scavenging black birds, we race up through scrawny timber to the bike path. My daughter follows with the delirious pup, chasing other big dogs and squirrels on the secret river path. Her boy weaves back and forth over the dotted yellow line, not in the right lane. Headfirst into a deep puddle, he expertly guns his pedals straight up the other side. Back at the beach, he tells Mummy he wants to climb higher onto the giant boulders forming the breakwater jetty. Riding onto the sandy beach, he learns his wheels won't turn there. Hungry and energized, he pulls his bike up the grassy knoll without our help. He races ahead of us to the car.

blowing goodbye kisses
he decides on nuggets for lunch
drive-through only

Winning the Battle, but Not the War

SOPHIE PAGÉ

· · · · · · · ·

I've been working from home since the lockdown began, but little has changed from my old routine, except that my new co-worker is an orange fuzzball named Calvin. I've had worse colleagues. When he's quiet and affectionate, I think that my situation isn't so bad, that I could get used to being stuck indoors with only a cat for company. But then there are moments when I remember why I usually prefer working in an actual office with other human beings.

I have a call with my boss in the late morning, and, while we're discussing production tracking, Calvin is on my lap attacking the cord of my earbuds. Every time I push him off, he jumps right back, oblivious to my frustration. He's having fun, so much so that my boss can hear him purring through the phone. "Is that your cat?" he asks. "He sounds like a lion." At one point, Calvin falls off my lap with the cord still in his mouth and yanks the earbuds out of my ears. Pleased with himself, he heads to his food bowl to slurp and grunt his way through his second breakfast before taking a well-earned nap.

Roused and refreshed, he decides to try his hand at acrobatics. Clearly, he was practicing his moves all the times I was away at the office. He balances precariously on the edge of the couch's armrest, then jumps in the air in a neat arc and lands on the kitchen counter. The first time he does it, I grab the spray bottle of water and spritz him. The second time, I jingle a box of coins until he jumps off. The third time, he leaps off the counter of his own volition but then gives me a look that says: *I do this whenever you're out of the room. You can't stop me.*

Maybe so, but I can try. After some brainstorming, I grab a couple of small, unused boxes from the back of a cupboard and arrange them along the edge of the counter. Calvin balances again on the armrest and stares at them. I can almost hear the little gears in his head spinning as he does the cat equivalent of recalculating the distance between himself and the counter. Whatever conclusions he comes to must not be to his liking, because he changes his mind and jumps off the couch. I assume that's the end of it.

Once the day is over, I head to the shower. While drying myself, I hear a *thunk* from the living room. I head out of the bathroom to find the boxes on the counter in disarray and Calvin sitting on the floor, meowing at me reproachfully. My trick worked. Today, I won the battle, but whether I win the war remains to be seen.

Murmuration

ILONA MARTONFI

· · · · · ● · · · ·

I meant to watch endless replays of you. Marisa. And so said: "How are you?"

"Okay."

The cell phone pictures of a bus driving up streets, houses of greystone and brick. Schools, libraries, bookstores, restaurants, weddings, funerals, a city in lockdown. Quarantine. I am afraid for you.

This cold spring day. This small lilac sky above the assisted living for seniors, retirement home for my eldest daughter. This seventh day of March. This swarm. This COVID-19 pandemic.

Do you remember finally moving to your own studio, on Avenue Caldwell near Chemin Kildare? Villa-Maria metro, bus 162. And so I said: "Do you like it?" Glassy detachment. Suffering from pulmonary sarcoidosis autoimmune disease. Your bouts of pneumonia. Psychiatric outpatient of St. Mary's Hospital. Generalized anxiety disorder. Daughter on public curatorship. Your three children who grew up without their mother.

I meant to keep packing and unpacking orange boxes. Meant just to watch your medications. Underline them. Put question marks behind them. And so you said: "I'm not like them. I am not." It's your monosyllables. Marisa.

"Marisella," your father called you. "My daughter is an artist," he said. "Babba," he called you. "Stupid."

At six, you stood up to him. "Stop hitting mama!" you said.

Fast food. Coke and French fries. Music on a black Boombox. All the different helpers in your life. It would be more than seven. And so you said: "I go to the Shopping Centre." "Which one?"

"Côte-Saint-Luc."

It's your monosyllables. Swooping starlings in murmuration.

Sounds like the ocean waves. Disappear at the end, like a phantom. Leaving everything else motionless.

A Scene from a Parking Lot at the End of the World

CHARLES GEDEON

. . . .

Maroun looks up into the bright sun. The cool wind across his stubbled cheek carries with it the memories of normalcy. Summer on the horizon should feel like hope and a fresh start.

Seagulls caw above the empty parking lot. Maroun smiles with one eye shut to block out the sun. His gaze follows the birds into the sky; when he looks back down, he notices an abandoned child's bike. A lone woman across the lot stares at the bike blankly. It's a fitting scene for a world hiding from a virus, he thinks. He closes his eyes, lowers his head, and listens as the wind begins to blow harder.

The unexpected sound of children's laughter prompts Maroun to open his eyes. He watches as a girl runs out from behind a hedge. She jumps on the once-lonely bike, and whizzes around a signpost that reads: "Arrêt." Her little brother chases her, laughing. The woman turns out to be an attentive but exhausted mother, watching from a safe distance.

Maroun smiles as he gets up. It's not every day a university parking lot is a playground at 5 pm.

The wind is colder. He puts his hands in pockets, feels for a keychain in the shape of a cedar tree, starts walking home. It's his turn to hide again.

Pandem Random Through One-Way Glass

RANA BOSE

· · · · · ● · ● · · ·

Who is this guy who steps out of a car called a Crossfire, wearing a maroon baseball cap and noise-cancelling headphones, carrying a large Coke bottle everyday at 1 pm?

Who is this frenetic lady, a woven basket on her back (like a tea-garden worker in Darjeeling), with an untrained but sweet, black Labrador, dragging her to a health food store every day, as she screams: "Stop! Stop!" interminably?

What is on the minds of these thirty-two-year-old, or maybe twenty-five-year-old joggers who chat, cough, and sneeze, unmasked, as they move along in their Lululemon tights, against the cytokine storm ahead?

Who is this fedora-ed man, whose beagle moves slightly faster than he does, tirelessly dragging his ears every day—until they both flop down on the same bench next to a bus stop?

Where did this unmasked family of four come from, the man with a tuque on and the woman with a flop-hat, and two toddlers who charge around in circles, run into the middle of the street, squealing and squeaking, while the parents giggle and fart—loudly?

Who are these two bearded men, stumbling along in black and plaid, with caps and masks—of a "vulnerable" age—and walking exactly two metres apart, one down the middle of the road, the other along the pavement?

***

He is a carpenter, working for cash in a house across the street. The coke bottle has no rum, he tells someone crudely into his phone. He eats a sandwich and a banana, slams the door shut, and goes back to work; as the anti-kickback shoulders of his saw whip back in, the sawdust explodes in his face.

She lived alone, somewhere far West, in a barn where the Symbionese Liberation Army once stockholmed Patty. She retreats further north, where plastic backpacks are banned, and dogs cry for raw meat and carrots, and horses have left the barn.

They are kitchen-less condo owners, who app-order food every night—and Oh! they apparently like *vindaloo* so much. They do trend-adjusted smoothening of exponential projection models—but these MF-rs are just clueless about the connections between big data, values, life, and the tempering of dried chilli and black mustard.

He has been living with Spencer (of Tracy's looks) for the last fifteen years, in a subsidized elderly care home, and the bus-stop bench, three blocks away, is their daily Zátopek moment.

This is an honest, non-swearing family from just a bit to the west of the city, headed for a park, where the yellow tape is already up and they don't know yet, and they will shout, scream, and cry, when they find out—and still fart. Because they have been betteraving, cabbaging, and bereaving every night, until CERB kicks in.

Those two are conversing about Sacco and Vanzetti.

COVID the Barbarians

ENDRE FARKAS

· · · · · · · · · ·

Wednesday, *April 1, 2020*
    Invisible as the air
they ride on our breath
coughs, sneezes
they are missiles
targeting knobs, cogs, skin
lungs, you name it.
This is the invisible world
manifesting its destiny
its fervour breaking through
But the truth is
we are the barbarians
who have been looting
and pillaging
clear cutting the way
for their release.
The truth is we are
the pandemic

Tai Chi Monday—April 6, 2020
Monday
Breathe
Monday
Commence
Monday
Tuck

Monday
Step
Monday
Centre
Monday
Raise arms
Monday
Form a ball
Monday
Turn
Monday
Part wild horse's mane
Part wild horse's mane
Part wild horse's mane
Monday
Half step in
Half step back
Monday
Spread white crane's wings
Monday
Brush knee
Brush knee
Brush knee
Monday
Half step in
Half step back
Play the lute
Monday
Repulse the monkey
Repulse the monkey
Repulse the monkey
Repulse the monkey
Monday
Protect high and low
Monday

Look up
Monday
Grasp the bird's tail
Monday
Almost touch
Monday
Clean off
Monday
Send bird back to nature
Monday
Turn
Monday
Protect high and low
Monday
Look up
Monday
Grasp the bird's tail
Monday
Almost touch
Monday
Clean off
Monday
Send bird back to nature
Monday
Single whip push
Monday
Wave hands like cloud
Wave hands like cloud
Wave hands like cloud
Monday
Single whip push
Monday
Single whip push
Monday
High pat the horse

Monday
Kick with right heel
Monday
Box opponent's ears
Monday
Turn, kick with left heel
Monday
Serpent in the grass
Monday
Golden rooster stands on left leg
Monday
Serpent in the grass
Monday
Golden rooster stands on right leg
Monday
Beauty works shuttles
Beauty works shuttles
Beauty works shuttles
Monday
Needle at sea bottom
Monday
Half step back
Monday
Push the moon away
Monday
Flash arms like a fan
Monday
Turn
Monday
Deflect
Monday
Parry
Monday
Punch
Monday

Shut the door
Monday
Scoop up energy
Monday
Cross hands
Monday
Half step in
Monday
Tuck
Monday
Close
Monday
Breathe

Thursday—April 9, 2020
Snow falling on spring
in numbers, individuals
become statistics
beautiful flakes alight
on skeletal branches
that just sprouted buds
a gray canvas of
bare balconies
curtained windows
rainbows and smiles
drawn by children
colour the coming night

PENNING THE PANDEMIC
We Can All Be Writers

NISHA COLEMAN

. . . .

I'm a writer, but I don't have much to say right now. I'm a storyteller, but I don't have many stories to tell either. There is an explosion of online content, but I do not feel compelled to contribute. Instead, I watch, listen, notice.

In week one of self-isolation measures, among the profusion of COVID-19 memes about toilet paper, face touching, and the chaos of quarantining with kids, one in particular caught my attention:

As an introverted writer (with a splash of agoraphobia), I realized that in many ways I'd been unwittingly adhering to a regime not unlike the #stayhome measures put in place in an effort to #flatten-thecurve. For years, I've been working alone at home in Montreal, sometimes not using my voice or emerging into the outside world for days at a time. Suddenly, much of the world was sharing some very specific elements of my solitary life, as expressed in a new slew of memes and statuses:

OMG. I'm wearing pants without an elastic waist today!
The days just run into one another, seems it hardly matters what day it is.
How many granola bars a day is reasonable?

Without an external force, it can be difficult to keep a handle on simple concepts like mealtimes, wearing actual pants, and being aware of the time or even the day of the week. I only started wearing jeans about a year ago; I consistently miss recycling day; and my "meals" are often just slices of toast with a rotation of spreads depending on where the sun is in the sky.

By week two of the #stay(thefuck)home directive, when it became clear that the two-week isolation period was just an appetizer for what was to come, I noticed another phenomenon. The already effervescent internet was exploding with content—a different kind of content. Hand-drawn cartoons. Spontaneous paintings. Live videos igniting at all hours. And music, from celebrity live streams to living room solo jam sessions. A clear and urgent desire to share. Not masterpieces, not carefully crafted content. Perfection wasn't the point. The point, it seemed, was simply connecting.

In her book, *The Lonely City: Adventures in the Art of Being Alone*, Olivia Laing writes, "If loneliness is to be defined as a desire for intimacy, then included within that is the need to express oneself and to be heard, to share thoughts, experiences, and feelings."

Maybe the isolation and loneliness of being a writer also fuels the force that compels me to create and share my work with the world.

Maybe a sort of collective loneliness was setting in, and, with it, the need to self-express. Maybe the isolation and loneliness of being a writer also compels me to create and share my work with the world. While my version of self-isolation is self-imposed, it doesn't mean it's not lonely. It very often is. And now, the rest of the world was lonely too, which I'll admit made me feel less lonely.

Week three, another shift. Things became darker. The funny memes slowed. Longer posts started to surface. Honest struggles. The isolation, among other hardships, was taking its toll. One widely-shared article features Keith LaMar, who has been in solitary confinement for the last twenty-seven years. "You have to learn how to deal with yourself," he counsels.

But facing the self can be terrifying.

Artists and writers are sometimes perceived as navel-gazing (one critic called my solo storytelling show, aptly titled *Self-Exile*, "solipsistic"). Often they are simply dealing with themselves, mining themselves for material, for in the specific can be found the universal.

As a memoir writer and true-life storyteller, I've been doing a lot of mining. If I were a limestone quarry, you could build a small village with the material I've dug up. LaMar points out that "educate" comes from "educe," which means to bring out or develop. His advice for those in isolation is to "bring forth that which is already there." Of course, what's "already there" can be a minefield of grief, abandonment issues, anxiety—things that are more comfortable left unexplored. Exploration can be excruciating, but also empowering. There is beauty waiting there too. And strength.

As the exterior world falls away, our rich inner world can come into focus. At a time when we would normally see social media inundated with pics of bathing suits and beaches in exotic locations, I was seeing something far more interesting, even exotic: expressions of quieter but complex selves. Someone noticed a blue jay flash by the window. Someone heard geese overhead. The moon has made a comeback. So much bread baked! So many puzzles! Photos displayed a bouquet of fresh parsley or leafless treetops against a moody sky, or a beam of sunlight spilling over a radiator. Selfies, instead of flattering filters, featured expressions of worry or sadness or a brave but tenuous smile.

I don't like the expression, "We're all in the same boat." I think of Noah's ark, hundreds or thousands or millions of people jammed together, heading to the same destination, seeing and experiencing the same thing. The image makes me shudder in these COVID times, but it doesn't sit right. As we experience this global phenomenon, we are forced to do so separately, as individuals. Instead of the same big boat, I picture individual rafts. We're all sailing, but at different speeds and on different bodies of water. Our rafts have slightly different designs; sometimes we get stuck, or find we've been going backward. We are alone on our raft, all paddling together. I think of my writer friends toiling away alone at their desks, deep in personal projects, but unified in our solitary toils.

We can all be writers. We have to be, if we don't want someone else to write the story.

And there is something else that writers do, maybe the best part—writers imagine. Different worlds. Different people and scenarios. The way things could be. Our world is changing drastically. We don't know what it will look like, which means there is room to imagine. How we want to be. What inner climate we want. What we can do to curb the outer climate. What kind of relationships we want to have. What kind of spaces we want to create. Unshaven, in our elastic-wasted PJs, primed to binge on granola bars and sipping a tenth cup of coffee, we can gaze out the window. We can imagine something new. Something different. Something beautiful.

At the End of Nowhere

BRENDA HARTWELL

. . . .

As the sun breaches the horizon, a chorus of chickadees, song sparrows, and robins greet the new day and my yearning ear. What day is it? So hard to keep track during this protracted period of isolation. What does it matter? There are no board meetings to attend, no workshops, no appointments, no luncheon dates. There is a certain freedom in this seemingly endless string of days.

Outside my kitchen window is a panorama: a frost-glittered field, apple trees ornamented with blue jays pecking at the stubborn remains of last year's harvest, the fallow garden, Lac Lyster in the distance with the rock-faced Pinnacle looming over it. We are here on a *cul de sac*, at the end of nowhere. The air is pure, the water potable, and there is space aplenty to roam. Residents here have no trouble keeping six—even twenty-six—feet apart.

A mother hen, I have gathered my chicks under my wing. My daughter and her new husband are both immune suppressed, so we have persuaded them to leave Montreal and return to the nest. The addition built when my son played drums is cordoned off, while they spend their fourteen days in total isolation. There will be no trips to the grocery store, no visits with friends, and certainly no hugs. My husband and I have been home, with no excursions to the village for over three weeks, so we are secure in the knowledge we are not infected. Groceries are delivered weekly and everything is washed with sudsy water. The drug store delivers too, although one of my rheumatoid arthritis drugs has become unavailable, a result of the uneducated ramblings of the orange incompetent president south of the border.

My days are full enough to keep me occupied. My pile of unread books is diminishing. Because there are no cooking facilities where my daughter is holed up, I plan, cook, and deliver vegetarian meals to the patio door. Empty dishes are deposited directly into a waiting pan of hot soapy water. The daily routine also includes walks down the gravel road to an uninhabited lake, a tranquil spot. Where the ice has pulled away from the shore, minnows are already in evidence. If I hanker for a longer amble, a logging road will take a soul deep into a woods of sugar maple. At home, our writing-group members take turns sending out prompts to inspire. We've rediscovered the phone. Cherished voices are a lifeline.

Trying to Work Here

DIDI GORMAN

· · · · · · · · ·

Is it morning yet? I open one eye and look at the clock. It's 7:17 am. Oh well, time to get up. What day is it, anyway?

The coffee helps me to remember: it's Tuesday. I head to my computer. As a writer who works from home, I'm working as usual. Or at least, I'm trying.

I sit down, sip my coffee, and open my email. I don't usually get much correspondence, but the past few days have seen a flood of email from various teachers and school boards informing us of the many platforms/resources/links/online projects our kids should/ could/may/must be doing in the coming weeks.

Thing is, I'm working. I can't possibly look at all this now, let alone supervise a homeschooling program. It's far too time-consuming. As a matter of fact, I'm writing an essay right now. It's pretty dystopian, if you ask me. What is it about? you ask. Ah! Two points, if you can guess! You guessed pandemic? Wow. I'm impressed. How could you possibly have known?

Anyway, I'm back at my essay. I've already written the first few lines. Time to start the second paragraph. *Life under quarantine is an unusual experience.* Oh! Hang on—an email just came in. Let me just check. It's another message from school with tips on how to tutor our children. I really can't read this now; it will have to wait. Where was I?

Life under quarantine is an unusual experience….

What's that? My Zoom is flashing. Someone has just sent me an invitation to a Zoom conference. I have a quick look and deem the invitation non-essential. Back to my essay.

Life under quarantine is an—

"Mommy, can you come help me with math?"

"Not now, sweetie. I'm working."

Okay, let's try this again. *Life under quarantine is an unusual experience. For sure, it makes it... uhm... For sure, it's...*

Who just sent me an invite to Facebook Live? It really couldn't have waited? I can't concentrate.

Life under quarantine is an unusual experience. For sure, it makes it almost impossible to focus on writing an essay about what an unusual experience life under quarantine is.

Headlines Before Gaslighting

ANITA ANAND

· · · · · · · · ·

I'm alarmed by everything everyone else is alarmed by, but I don't mind working from home, because—introversion. I don't miss commuting, dealing with difficult people, experiencing the tangible, physical pressure of groups of students. Feeling blessed: my husband's home too. He rescues me from techno-bugs when I teach online.

No emails from work. I spot *Medium Daily Digest* and read that instead. Contributor Julio Vincent Gambuto writes: "Prepare for the ultimate gaslighting." He warns that governments and corporations will try to make us forget what suddenly became clear during this "pause." He predicts a feel-good advertising campaign will begin as the crisis ends, to distract us from what we've seen.

And what have we seen?

Headlines I've been collecting:

Roadkill dramatically decreases.

Coyotes spotted on the Golden Gate Bridge.

Blue skies in Los Angeles.

Giant pandas mate at an empty zoo.

Roadside grass won't be trimmed this year: rare wildflowers flourish.

Deer take over East London streets.

Giant turtles seen at Versova beach in Mumbai, first time in twenty years.

It's as if Mother Nature said: "Okay, you assholes. Enough already with all this mindless driving and flying around." On TV, Boucar Diouf, explaining how viruses work, offhandedly mentions that, in the sea, if one organism grows too dominant, a virus appears to control its population.

But "controlling population"? That's so cold.

Mass grave trenches dug in New York City.

Bodies left in the streets of Ecuador.

I think of my mother, who is disabled and currently dependent on the kindness and caution of strangers.

Which brings me to the other thing we've seen.

So much love. A kind of collective consciousness of love. I cut short a walk past the pastel rainbows to call my mother. Bing! Two emails simultaneously arrive from friends asking about her.

She says she's okay, that her phone never stops ringing. She admits the number of deaths involving seniors is concerning. Her various caregivers work in different residences—but they do wear masks.

Her meals are being delivered to her; the dining room's been closed for a month. When she asks the staff, they say nobody is sick. She finds that suspicious, because, "we're all old and sick here." Also, she misses going downstairs for a cookie whenever she feels like having one.

I want a cookie. I don't do grocery shopping anymore. My husband goes and wears my black ski mask. I'm Indian; when I wear it, I get hateful looks, or at least imagine them.

My husband laughs when I tell him, but he agrees to go. Soon. How long can I wait for a cookie?

The doorbell rings. The mailbox *thunks* open and shut.

Our lovely friend, Christine, is already at the bottom of the steps, grinning like a kid.

I open the paper bag. Chocolate chip shortbread!

I blow her a kiss.

And I go inside thinking: *I touched a paper bag, then brought my fingers to my mouth.*

But all the sugar, butter, and kindness have a way of distracting me.

Rallying to Meet the Challenge

ELIZABETH GLENN-COPELAND

. . . .

Late morning finds me sitting in my chair, coffee in hand, staring out the window and marvelling at how, in four short weeks, our life has been turned upside down.

In early March, we were with our friends in Milles-Isles, days away from signing the papers on what was to be the home in which we would end our years on this beautiful earth. Then COVID-19 hit, our 2020 income took flight, and, with it, the dream for our home in the woods. These past few years have seen a sudden surge of interest in my husband's music, producing an income sufficient for us to make this move. But two nights ago, his manager informed us not to expect any income until May 2021. Like many senior artists, we don't have big pensions or savings, so we have enough money to last through the summer. Thanks to the kindness of strangers, we have a place to stay for free until the state of emergency lifts, at which point we are looking at driving out of here with our cats and what we can essentially pack in our car.

So, as you can imagine, this past week has been a dizzying dance to rally and meet the challenge, interspersed with fits of crying. But today, knowing that many artists are in similarly dire circumstances, I have rallied. I have made a list of what will be required to get through the next few months. I have actively prayed for those in need, and for the health of those we love and cherish, some of whom are in Montreal and Toronto, all hard hit by COVID-19. I spent the first hours of the morning writing a letter of encouragement to artist friends, then made a tenuous peace with the very real possibility that, as our home equity may be required to feed and house us through the next winter, we will never again have a home.

Once I finish this letter, I will heat up the beef stew prepared by a young couple in the town, without whose help we could not manage. I will snuggle with my cat, do my qigong practice, stand out under the sky, and give thanks for the beauty that the Mother continues to provide. I will polish and send off a poetry submission, then line up a few cheery romantic comedies to enjoy with my husband.

I have known for years these times were coming. We had hoped to be hunkered down somewhere safe near friends with access to clean water and forest in which to worship, but it didn't turn out that way. No amount of wailing will make it so. So I say to myself and all of you...

Have courage! We are the bards, the tellers of stories that heal the collective heart. We will pass through the eye of this needle and prevail.

Leaving My Runners Behind

JOSH QUIRION

. . . .

Loafing.

I belong to a blessed faction of Canadian citizenry that remains employed.

And what's more, I have the luxury of completing my work remotely from the relative comfort of my one-bedroom apartment. Although I recognize that my circumstances might be more favourable than those of others, I cannot but shake my head when I think of the seventh floor.

And of what I left there.

A month ago, the corporation that pays my bills tele-booked forty or so cabs and sent home a string of employees, with all the office equipment they could carry on their backs, for an undetermined duration.

It was raining, and as I stood on the sidewalk at the intersection of Maisonneuve and Guy with my dual-monitors, wireless keyboard and mouse, and other ergonomic office paraphernalia, I realized I had forgotten my running shoes seven floors above.

Whatever, I thought. I'll be back soon enough. Just go home; it's raining.

Besides, I couldn't recall the last time I'd derived real gratification from jogging. As a matter of fact, I couldn't recall the last time I'd actually jogged.

But—what if, just in case....

Today, in an act of desperation, I laced up an old pair of leather Ralph Lauren loafers with two eyelets on either side—four eyelets less than the Nike Roshe running shoes, which remain seven floors above the ghostly downtown boulevard.

I ran to the office.

Taking Notice in a "Stopped" World

KARIN TURKINGTON

· · · · · · · · ·

As an introvert, I'm managing quite well with all this alone time. I love the quiet.

I listen to CBC radio, so I feel like I'm not really alone. Normally, I'd be woken up by the sound of car alarms and trucks bumbling down the street over potholes. This quiet is a rare treat, and I'm grateful for it. I can hear the birds singing and the occasional sound of children and families playing outside.

Since the weather has become milder, I would like to ride my bike, but government restrictions seem to forbid it, so I've left it in storage where it's been all winter. I sit far too much in front of my laptop, watching educational YouTube Videos and Netflix, but I also keep writing and organizing my e-files of poetry and stories. Maybe I could even finish some of them!

I've participated in a couple of Zoom group meetings; however, it's just not the same as meeting in person. I end up feeling invisible.

I text my two daughters regularly: one in Montreal and the other in Toronto. My Toronto daughter has a two-month-old boy, so I reach out to her quite often. She sends me pictures of baby Theo almost daily. I wish I could cuddle him. Luckily, I was able to meet him when he was a couple of weeks old.

I'm reading Heather O'Neill's novel, *Lullabies for Little Criminals*. I'm loving it!

I would like to repaint my apartment a luscious bright white and my bedroom a muted eggplant shade. I've used this colour before in a bedroom. It's calm and reassuring.

From the time I was a child, I used to wonder why the world didn't stop when bad things happened to people, animals, and places. Why did life just go on as if nothing at all happened? At last, I know what it feels like to be in a "stopped" world. We have no choice but to take notice. No one can buy their way out of this. So I feel a levelling that I've never known before—a levelling that makes us all equal. Vulnerable. I certainly feel more equal than I ever did. This makes me feel strangely calm. We really are all the same, in the face of this virus.

Today, I'm going to do some sewing and practise random machine embroidery. I love textiles, not only for the clothes they can become, but for the art pieces into which they may evolve. As always, I will continue to work on making my tiny apartment as beautiful as possible.

On the Desire to Be Authentic

MORGAN COHEN

· · · · · · · · ·

Distressed, I stumble off the pebbled path. Avoiding the mud, I climb onto a large rock, my rustic Blundstone boots squeaking and pressing into my shins. I am eye to eye with a cow. As I step up to get a closer look at her curious, fearful eyes, she hastily retreats backward. I glance behind me at the herd for—encouragement? Validation? They immediately avert their gaze. I sigh, understanding their distrust. I lean my body against the wooden fence, stretch my arms out, allow them to go limp along the uneven surface.

As the cows slowly and carefully approach me, my thoughts drift to the gaze piercing my back. My fellow kibbutz volunteers, their contempt, momentarily leaves me breathless. I note the absence of physical pain and remind myself not to feed what the coronavirus has revealed—the fear of the unknown. Before the outbreak, I chose to spend a few months on a kibbutz, drawn by the promise of slowness and simplicity, a chance to understand myself better, free from the impositions of capitalist society. But ideology, like bacteria, is not contained by borders. Here, your passport dictates your identity: the German—stringent; the South African—imperial; the American (CANADIAN)—entitled. Histories, cultures—these are simplified and polarized to fit a pattern. Feeling caged, I want to lash out, scream. But I am silent, rejecting the role of the spectacle, refusing to let fear engulf me. I chase away these thoughts and attempt to focus on what's before me.

The cows gnaw at my distressed denim jacket. I question my fascination with these animals. I look down at my boots—my cheeks burn. My isolation from the human herd makes me very aware of my appearance: my designer aviators, which sit gently on my nose, become heavier. Soft hands grip the rough wood; my speech wavers. Guilty about my inheritance, the implications of my last name, I'm surprised with myself for succumbing to the superficiality of the state's expectations. My desire to have the right clothing, the right accent—to blend in, so that, in this time of uncertainty, I won't have the habitual finger pointed in my direction, condemning my take on the world.

I close my eyes and take a deep breath, acknowledging that I can only maintain this appearance for so long. Desiring to be authentic—whatever that entails—I breathe deeply. I say good-bye to the cows, knowing I'll return without an audience the following day. I leap from the mound into a muddy concoction, then wipe the shit off—I break away from the herd, the impositions, the stereotypes. I acknowledge that my search for rhythm amid the chaos will be difficult, but I relish the challenge.

When Night Falls

RACHEL BERGER

. . . .

Tonight, I read a book. At 8 pm, my kids were tired and happy at the end of another day spent entirely in the company of their moms. Their moms, who never had time, suddenly have nothing but, and our six-year-old twins are relishing it. They are also leery of this set-up, nostalgic for what they are starting to understand they might have lost: progress in the game they were playing at school, the unlikeliness of seeing their quirky friend ("he can't remember my name, so he calls me 'bro,' but I am not his brother!"), chess club on Thursdays. They want to know what the eff is going on. When will they go back to school? When will the moms stop being so available? We don't know. We reassure them that everything is fine, but we fail to offer anything satisfying. We put them to bed at 8 pm without fail.

And then we veg. Most nights, we gesture toward togetherness; we want to want to be together, but actually we just want to be alone—alone with snacks and escapist media. We re-watch shows and films we know by heart, finding comfort in our absolute certainty of what comes next. We stay up too late, as if this were a vacation, as if tomorrow will yield some relief from the monotony and dread of this limbo.

Last week, I cycled between dysregulation and dissociation. I spent my evenings obsessively putting together a 1000-piece puzzle made up mostly of three monochromatic colours. The light was dim, heightening my ardour for the task. It was great.

Today, I felt better, good enough to read. I picked up *In The Dream House* by Carmen Maria Machado, served well by a story written in vignettes. It relays the violent end to the romance of two young women, but I am not yet at the end. I am still at the beginning, full of desire and the bodies that yield to it, dirty sex in shitty housing, the bluster of young ambition. I am transported to places where I have been nothing but free: driving in a car with a lover in an unfamiliar country, the radio blasting, her hand moving up my thigh, governed only by petrol and radio reception, on the road to nowhere. It all came crashing down, as the story will in the novel, but the essence of it was the freedom we felt before the fall.

Soon it will be time to sleep and then wake into the new day. Tomorrow is April 7, day twenty-six of this lockdown. There will be inquiries about breakfast by 7 am, the need for structure and schooling by 9 am, then snacks, and meals, and more play, and more snacks, another meal. We will run the dishwasher a hundred times, do one thousand loads of laundry. But night will fall again, and who knows what it may offer up, if we can rise to meet it.

Living with Bedbugs: Give Me COVID

KATE HENDERSON

· · · · · · · · · ·

It's the end of March in Montreal and an unexpected four inches of snow covers the ground. I walk along the riverside before starting my work-from-home day. The birds are quiet, the current moves sluggishly, snow lines the branches.

Quebec Premier François Legault has announced that we have until midnight to get what we need. It's not until I'm heading back to my apartment that I remember my biggest problem isn't COVID-19.

It's bedbugs. And my exterminators are not considered essential services. They called last night to say they could fit me in some time between 9 am and midnight. I'm thankful they didn't cancel, but how will I explain a six-hour absence from Zoom meetings while the chemical fumes dissipate? There's nowhere else to get a connection; I cannot say I have an appointment. Internet cafés, libraries, doctors' offices—all closed.

I could stand with my laptop at the coin-operated dryer in the basement. I know I can get a signal down there, because I checked. But six hours is a long time, and how hot will it get if someone needs the machines?

I've been social distancing for months. I avoid friends' houses, because no matter how much they love you, no one wants bedbugs. I don't want to take a chance that one has burrowed into a crevice of my sole.

All of my belongings have tumbled in the dryer at high heat. Every week, I wash sheets and blankets. Every morning, I dress in clothes sealed in plastic bags. Surely, I think, I'm overdoing this. Surely, the chemicals the exterminators spray around my apartment, upending mattresses and bedframes in visits carefully timed to accommodate a bedbug's life cycle, will take care of things.

And then I'll find a rogue bug on my blanket, or scuttling across the floor.

I took this well-priced sublet to get my bearings after the breakdown of my marriage. Almost a year later, three months into a new job, the bedbug saga began. I didn't tell work colleagues, because I saw the looks on the faces of my friends.

I call when I know my ex will be sitting at his desk, drinking his morning cup of coffee. Graciously, he says yes, I can come and set up at his apartment. When? I tell him I don't know.

At 9 am, the exterminator pulls up outside. He's over six feet, dressed in black leather, a spray gun and canister swinging at his side. Under normal circumstances, I might consider this man mildly dangerous, but today I smile when I see his familiar gait in the hallway. He's the only person to enter my apartment for months.

When I get to the place I used to live with my ex, it is quiet, orderly, and safe. Remembering, I breathe in the life we lived through two children and thirty years. It seems fitting to be exactly here, at this unusual moment in time.

Ça va bien aller....

You're Fine... You're Fine

SIVAN SLAPAK

. . . .

You're fine. You're still working and grateful. Safe in your apartment. You hear the jokes people are making about their living situations—how many will tramp to divorce lawyers after this, or the exhaustion of homeschooling. Living alone, you float through, quiet, relieved, sullen.

On your own, all your best and worst traits go unchecked: your idle isolation or your good intentions; your need for purpose, bordering on pushy (Let me help you, please. PLEASE.); your people-pleasing, self-doubt tipping into timorousness. Adding question marks to every sentence of a text, until a fleeting exchange becomes a hand-wringing formulation of "Is that okay?" "Are you okay?" "Are we okay?" Your voice constricts with emotion in a staff Zoom meeting for no reason, except—"Will it be okay?"

You're fine.

You're fine—but distracted.

Waiting in line outside the supermarket, you reach into your purse with chapped hands to find that you've accidentally packed your potholders instead of your wallet. You want to laugh or cry, catch someone's lifted eyebrows over a mask, maybe a smile: "Isn't this all absurd?"

You lie in bed with your anxiety buzzing around, ready to land on missed details of the day—a phone call you didn't make, a question mark you didn't add—circling away from larger questions you can't face.

You wonder if you'll ever touch someone again. You mourn the salsa course you finally took in the winter, clasping hands with a

116

series of strangers for eight Tuesdays, palms on your back steering you across the floor. In the last class, another student noted your ardent expression and remarked, "You love to dance." You felt shy, caught revelling. Yes. Then the spring session was cancelled.

You worry that things you cherish are non-essential. You think about the word *essential* constantly. You poke at every feature of your life, asking: "Is this essential?"—the way followers of Marie Kondo ask: "Does this spark joy?" You've lived lean before, learned to pare down, but you realize there's nothing left you'd want to give up.

You once had a job leading movement sessions for seniors with dementia; you carried to the residence a stack of CDs reflecting youth lived elsewhere. You could see who liked to dance, but also who had always loved it—an arrhythmic nod versus that glimmer you recognize. You watch as one struggles out of a chair to grip your hand and shuffles to a beat.

"You love to dance," you exclaim. *Oh yes!* Their voice, bolder than yours. Speaking about it, you'd describe it as someone's "essential self" revealed. However brittle the body or foggy the mind, that self remains, popping up as young as ever with the flick of a stereo switch. You gloried easily at a careful waltz through a residence living room smelling of bleach.

Old age. Will it matter that once a week some well-meaning caregiver takes a moment for a salsa step, delighting in your somatic memory? It seemed valuable at the time, but now the essentials of preserving life have a spare, consuming definition.

Hill Seeker

AIMEE LOUW

· · · · · · · ·

I'm that hill seeker in town
You may have seen me dressed up for winter on top and summer
on the bottom
Or dressed for spring on top, with yellow gloves and winter boots,
good to minus thirty
It's all possible
You may have noticed how I rig up my sun hat so it stays on, even
at top speed
—Well, sometimes.
You may have seen me flash by, unmatched colours and mixed woven
textures from behind the safety of your triple panes
I'm the hill seeker,
Down, circle around, and then back up only to come the fuck back
down again
Gravel trips
Who needs weed or drinks when you can leave it all behind at the top?
—Or is at the bottom?
And what is *it*, anyway?
What do *I* have to leave behind?
...
Years of loneliness
Needed to work from home
Not wanting to work from home
Years of ever present fear that I'll never survive on my own
Years of annual Christmas parties sitting through old aunts: *J'espère*
vraiment que tu trouverais ton emploi cette année

Look at what happens when the people deemed productive need
support—
when the workers become "needy":
suddenly programs pop up within a month
Gravel trips
Rock covered lips threaten to stall my chair
Threaten a good catapult through the air
And there, my dears,
Is the thrill
Oh—and there's that other hill!

Hold That Time, Please

DAN DAVID

· · · · · ● · · · ·

Thursday morning. The clock shows 7:14 am. I wouldn't care what day it is, except today is recycling day. Strangely, my cat didn't bust into my room at 6 am. Usually, she demands to be fed promptly at that hour. Not anymore, and I think I know why.

Houdini, named after an even greater escape artist, has a sense of time that isn't based on the rising sun, or some magical connection to Greenwich. The annual changes from Standard to Daylight Savings and back again never seem to faze her—until now, that is. Houdini's clock is off.

I think she once knew it was time to wake me up when the dog next door started barking during his 6 am morning run outside. She might've taken the cue from the cars rushing by, about the time people headed off to work. None of that happens anymore. Everything's quiet at 6 am, and has been so for a month.

I tuned into *Saturday Night Live At Home*, just in time to catch the end of Tom Hanks' opening monologue. He was, of course, in his empty kitchen. Something he said caught my attention: "There are no Saturdays anymore. It's all just today."

A post came across my Twitter feed the next day. It read: "I just realized it's Sunday." It generated dozens of "likes" and retweets in just a few hours. There was more than a little humour in those words. There was truth.

I think people related to Hanks' monologue and that tweet, because our concepts of time have been put on hold, if not altered forever. Blame the great lockdown that began in earnest, just as we sprang forward to Standard Time. Overnight, everything went quiet.

What difference would it make if it were Tuesday or Thursday, Saturday or Sunday? I found I didn't hate Mondays anymore. Even some monthly bills with their insistent reminders of impending doom were allowed to slide.

I dropped out of the rat race a decade ago, so it affected me less, I suppose. As a self-employed freelancer (read "mostly unemployed"), I've kept odd hours. I wake at 2 am to water the plants, or peck at the keyboard to exorcize stubborn demons. I no longer dance to the beat of a universal metronome. My time meanders like a stream, instead of running like a highway. I still reach my destination but enjoy the journey more.

I don't have kids. Eat when and what I want. Don't need to shop for a family. Can take a walk, listen to music, read a book without interruption. But like everyone under virtual house arrest, I need a schedule for the little things. Make the bed, do the laundry, wash the dishes. Without a little bit of structure, things that give me joy lose their meaning.

I guess it's time to get up and feed the cat. For some reason, something Groucho Marx once said comes to mind:

"Time flies like an arrow. Fruit flies like a banana."

Cheese Freeze and Canned Spinach

AUDREY MEUBUS

. . . .

This morning, I googled "is it okay to freeze cheese?" in an attempt to beat the expiration date.

My partner tried calling Service Canada for the 700th time. The call always disconnects before he's even had a chance to say a word to anyone on the line. I know better than to ask if I can help. All we can do is wait.

Today, I googled "recipes with canned spinach," and chose a few at random to consider. I don't know why I chose canned spinach at the grocery store two weeks ago. It seemed like a smart thing to do at the time.

I am thankful to have found a job that fills my days. I help dispatch content to streaming platforms, an essential service in times of confinement. I work long hours from home during the week. I miss sunlight. I take vitamin D every day to compensate.

The cats have been fighting constantly. They only just met a couple of months ago, and they are already sick of each other. There isn't enough space in this apartment for the four of us together. I can understand their frustration. The air is getting thin in here.

I seek personal space outside. I go for walks. I avoid other people, because that's what we're supposed to do. I cross paths with an older man without a mask. He doesn't step aside, so I wander into the street.

My comedian friend in Ojai sends jokes via text message: *How do you make holy water? You boil the hell out of it.* I deeply appreciate her grounded simplicity in these very serious times. I send her a heart emoji, because that's all I can muster in response these days.

My artist friend and I started building a virtual farm together in Stardew Valley. She was laid off from a job she loves because of the crisis. I'm selfishly glad that she doesn't have to go to work, because I get to speak to her more. I'm mostly relieved to know that she's safe.

I go on Twitter again, even though I promised myself I wouldn't anymore. I like some funny one-liners and then become sucked into a rabbit hole of COVID-19 deniers. I wonder what it must be like to live in denial. I consider this option for a moment. I log out.

We gather for our nightly ritual of dinner and what-should-we-do. We started a puzzle over the weekend, but it turned out to be too much of a commitment. We talk about the future and what may be left of it. We're guardedly optimistic. Home cooking helps.

We have made a nest for ourselves on the couch with blankets. The cats are asleep in their respective corners. We hold each other as we watch a Youtube video of a person walking through the streets of Kuala Lumpur. It helps to know that the world is still out there.

Before falling asleep, I google "how flat is the curve now?" in the hope that things would be better.

We're not quite there yet.

We have quite a few more days like this ahead of us.

PENNING THE PANDEMIC
Writer's Block in the Time of Corona

CAROLYN MARIE SOUAID

· · · · · • • · · ·

In mid-March, COVID-19 was getting out of hand, according to Premier Legault. There was too much handholding, not enough handwashing. I was sent home on a paid, two-week hiatus, while they rejigged my job to allow me to work from the confines of my condo.

Wait, what?

Yep, just like that, on a silver platter, I was handed a free writer's residency, a sort of Banff Centre—without the view. I arrived home buzzing with plans to return to my novel, a second attempt at an intimidating, mind-consuming genre, a labyrinth that is brutal to navigate under the best of circumstances. At last, I had the time I needed to drift, daydream, open myself up to the Muse.

Bright and early the next morning, I dug up my notes, twenty or so pages of rough dialogue, my character studies. And... waited, with my fat mug of coffee, as writer's block settled in. Nothing was coming except heartburn and anxiety. I made a sideways leap and brought out my sketchbook and charcoals. Maybe a different discipline would trigger something. It did.

I googled "online drawing tutorials." I learned about gesture and line of action. I drew stick figures and flour-sack torsos, filled my book with two-minute poses, not all bad. My humanoid sketches earned many "likes" from my Facebook friends.

By April 1, I came to realize that I was the Fool, having pissed away that free time—that subsidized residency that some only dream about. I was back at work—at home—on my regular hours, alone in my nine hundred-square-foot condo, except for the virtual humans congregating on Zoom. Something tugged inside: contrition, or maybe the grim reality of our collective isolation. We could be in this for months. If so, I would accrue the odd minute here and there, lulls in the day when they came up. Hours saved on the daily commute would amount to several weeks, enough for a jumpstart on the novel I'd seldom had time for. There were no excuses.

I re-read my writing. The protagonist materialized in my peripheral vision, strange indeed during this period of physical distancing. Other characters came forward, partly developed, with habits and idiosyncrasies. They joined me for dinner, watched me at the mirror brushing my teeth. Their voices spoke to me again.

Full disclosure: I'm a sucker for talking heads and messy lives, human sensibilities rubbing up against each other, bleeding all over the place, nudging a story forward. I prefer character-driven prose to something conceived on a rigid timeline. I like shaking hands with my characters, inviting them in, luggage and all. It's how I discover what they want, how they speak to each other, their strengths and weaknesses. This material is the engine for my story.

That night, I found a Myers-Briggs personality test online and administered it to my characters, as well as a questionnaire I use to help me build backstory. What's your favourite vegetable? If you were an animal, what would it be? When was your last orgasm? My iPhone and I settled into bed for another night in this Great April Fool's Joke the universe is playing on us. I loaded my favourite podcast: "Where Should We Begin? With Esther Perel." Essentially, you're a fly on the wall during family/couples' therapy. Why did this man cheat, or that woman not want children? Each podcast illuminates something about human nature and helps me create the emotional portfolios of my own characters. Helps me locate the details that shape them into the flesh-and-blood people we see—or, rather, used to see—huddled at the bus stop. Talking to each other. Holding each other.

Playing COVID Telephone Tag

MAUREEN MAROVITCH

• • • • • • • •

For the fourth day in a row, my husband calls his mother, Martha. The phone rings—eight, nine, ten times—with no answer.

A week ago, he received a call from the head nurse to say that Martha had a fever and cough. She was being tested for COVID-19. They were sedating people on her floor to keep them in their rooms. It's necessary, she explained. In the Alzheimer's unit, people wander into other rooms at all times of the day and night, mistake the startled occupant of the room for their dead spouse and try to kiss them, or lie down on a bed with someone in it and fall asleep.

It's Martha's fifth month in a nursing home, and we'd been asking to get her moved to another floor for the past several weeks. She has vascular dementia, which took her short-term memory, leaving her unable to retain what happened five minutes earlier; miraculously, it left intact her lively wit, her impressive vocabulary honed by decades of completing *The Globe and Mail* crossword, and her appreciation for art and music that she can't discuss with anyone on her floor. Many people there have forgotten how to speak English, if they ever knew how, and some are at the stage where they only yell or murmur incoherently. The head nurse had said they were looking for a better unit for her, but the virus shut down the search, along with all outside visits. We took some comfort in knowing that her lack of short-term memory would mean she wouldn't realize no one had visited in a while.

On the third day, the head nurse called back. Martha had tested positive, but her fever had gone down, and she was feeling better. She'd even eaten her lunch. We marvelled at this news over the phone with my father-in-law, alone in his apartment for the fourth week. Yes, Martha was eighty-five, but, aside from a hip and shoulder replacement, she was in good physical health. Even in her age bracket, most people survived the virus, we agreed. She was over the hump.

But then there was that silence again. For days after the diagnosis, no one answered the phone—not Martha, not the nursing station, not the administration. And then, after the Herron nursing home's massive death toll made national news, a perky medical student called us. No, she hadn't seen Martha or even met her; she wasn't allowed on that floor. She didn't know much except she had a message to convey to us that Martha was fine.

"Can you find out why she's not answering her phone?" we asked. She promised to email the nursing station.

Three pm on Sunday, we call for what must be the twelfth time in four days—and Martha answers. She can't tell us why she hasn't picked up the phone for a week. We learn she's used her walker, which must mean the phone has been out of reach, across the room. We hear shouting; she can't hear well, so we shout; she gets angry and yells back. But she's up and answering the phone, a week after being diagnosed with COVID-19. That feels like a tiny miracle.

No Sounds of Silence
in the Time of COVID-19

CAROL KATZ

After Simon & Garfunkel's The Sound of Silence

· · · · · · · · ·

This time silence has no sound.
A post-apocalyptic town.
People staying in their homes,
thinking about their health and woes
when social-distancing is the norm,
nowhere to roam.
Abandoned to the birds and pigeons.
And the people bowed and prayed
that the cure won't be delayed.
Worshipping from indoors
to Gods like mine and yours.
Voices sharing sounds
From distant lands
not holding hands
To the sound of silence.
No restaurants are open now
No swimming in a row.
Where do I get exercise?
Walking in the sun is wise.
But keeping two metres
from my friends,
wave my hands,

slowing the spread
of the Corona Virus.
Through silent streets
I walk alone,
staring at the cobblestones.
People standing at their windows
wanting company at their doors.
But the silence of the streets
are cold and damp, dark is the lamp,
whispering in the sound of silence.
One day, we'll all be well,
silence sounding like a bell.
I'll walking on busy streets,
people's faces smiling to the beat
of songs that are flowing from their lips, with a kiss,
Embracing the end of the Corona Virus.

A Time To Bless And Reassess

ANN LLOYD

· · · · · · · · · ·

Now trapped at home
look back, look back
on happy days
and then compute
as I was told so many years ago
with marriage
60/40 is okay
40/60 not so much
So recheck your coming freedom soon
And let your joyous happy days
Exceed the rest
Plan ahead and reassess
Then you'll be blessed

An Afternoon in Week 5

BARBARA KELLY

· · · · · · · · ·

B ody on a couch
blue blanket, pulled up close
photographs long ignored
faces on the table, in boxes,
rejects on the floor.
Pink tulips thirsty
or just tired.
TV buzzing news.

Outside, barren branches
large patches of snow
in slow retreat
murky grass, last year's leaves,
a dark squirrel nibbles.

Body rolls over
stands
walks to the kitchen
crackers, chips, wine,
phone,
iPad once more
chopped-onion tears

TV buzzing news:
transmission, lack of equipment,
the rising curve, expert opinions,

the pleas
of politicians.

And the journalists,
body's new friends
with bags under their eyes,
despite the make-up.

Dehydrated, soiled, abandoned,
the elderly are dying
despite it all.

One Week In

JEFFREY MACKIE-DEERNSTED

· · · · · ● · · · ·

Fragile emotions. New instructions every hour.
No hands touched
Digital counter on the population
Sunlight
Surfaces at the end of winter
Salted concrete dried crusts concrete not bread
Amusements grow old quickly
As we grow old slowly
On the TV
Sixteen Candles, Breakfast Club, Pretty in Pink
Relive your adolescence
With your significant other
That would be just ducky.

Plague

JOCELYNE DUBOIS

· · · · ● · · · ·

We sit two metres apart
I doodle & have naps in the afternoon
The phone rings more
friends checking in
some lonely
"Be safe" they say "be safe"
I need prescriptions renewed
dental check-ups
all cancelled
The streets are deserted
but grocery stores crowded
no pasta left on the shelves
We will get through this, I tell myself
with help from internet & phone
I read more
paint more
cook more
write more
I listen to you

Survival Plan

TANYA BELLEHUMEUR-ALLATT

. . . .

Wake up early.
       Write a poem.
Let it have angst, but also,
give the poem hope,
like a sticky drop
of maple syrup.
Drink it
like an elixir.
Enjoy it
for a moment.
Let it linger
like the cinnamon scent
of cider warming
on the wood stove.
Think about
tomorrow's poem
while you walk
along the road
with the dog.
Greet the birds,
newly returned.
Listen to them.
Gather all this
in your heart
like a round, white stone
tucked into your pocket

or a raven's feather
in your buttonhole.
Treasure it.
And then,
tomorrow morning,
begin again.

The Art of Jumping Cardboard Boxes

AMIE WATSON

· · · · · · · · ·

The highlight of my evening was jumping on a cardboard box. I had tried to rip it up, but there was a thick layer of tape across the bottom, and my nails are short.

Instead of getting scissors or a knife to break the box into pieces, I turned it upside down on the floor in the hallway and stepped on top of it while wearing my moccasin-style slippers, until it collapsed in slow motion. Then, I stepped up on the parts that were still sticking up, until they slowly folded inward too. After that, to get the last bits of resistant cardboard to submit to my wishes, I jumped. And jumped. And jumped. And smiled. It was like a bouncy castle for adults, but without the germs, which is important in this time of injunctions to "wash your hands, don't touch your face."

I was glad my neighbours didn't come out of their apartment to see what the commotion was—mostly out of fear of proximity, rather than embarrassment.

The other day, I went for a walk around my neighbourhood. I peeked into nearby apartments. I wanted to know how other people are living through this. Self-isolation is unique, depending on whether you're a parent of three, a sixty-year-old living alone, or a student with roommates.

Are they smiling? Are they bored? Are they experimenting with sourdough? Are they jumping on boxes? I wondered. Are they having one-person dance parties to the "Mood Booster" playlist on Spotify? Is that everyone's default "suggested for you" playlist these days, or does Spotify know that I'll probably like Chelsea Cutler and

Alexander 23's "Lucky"? Does it know I'm living alone? (Is Spotify making me paranoid?)

As I walked by one open window, I saw three twenty-something roommates sitting in a living room together, two sharing a couch and one on a chair, each on his laptop. I was jealous. They have other people. I can't invite friends over. I'm not sure I'm supposed to be running with anyone else, even if we keep two metres between us and shout our news at each other—it is still the highlight of my day, far better than box jumping.

I want to find out what people's lives are like. Are they changing their shirts every day? Putting on pants? Giving blood? Taking up running? Did they buy the last pull-up bar before I could? I've started wearing spring dresses at home as an excuse to keep this from turning into a leggings or pyjamas fest. Besides, it's warmer indoors than out.

As I (not-so-seriously) consider doing my taxes for the third time, just for something to do, and mess up trial #1 of a cinnamon amaretti recipe for an article I'm writing, I wonder how long this will continue. How many more living rooms will I get to peek into? How many more still lifes will I walk past?

More importantly, when will I actually be invited in?

Maintaining the Communications Flow

TIFFANY CROTOGINO

· · · · ● · · · ·

It's Monday, again. (It could be Tuesday, or Thursday, or every second Saturday—it would be the same story.)

The pandemic has changed my routine only slightly. I get to linger a little longer with my morning coffee and fuss a little less over what to wear. (These days, it's Casual Friday every day.) I still pack a lunch and head off to work. The traffic has been exceptionally light, making the commute an easy one.

I leave my seventy-seven-year-old mother and my eighteen-year-old son to hold the fort. We moved in mid-February, and so we aren't sure what "normal" is in our new house-neighbourhood-community. We all agree that the "current normal" isn't quite what we had planned.

Mom dutifully sanitizes all high-touch surfaces twice a day since, despite all appropriate precautions, we don't know what I might bring home with me. She sews beautiful masks out of quilting cottons, for us and for the extended family (delivered by Canada Post). My son mostly keeps to his new, electronic man cave in the basement—online classes, online assignments, online friends, online play—except when he's out running. He's an athlete, but he has never been much of a runner until now. Now he keeps distance and time targets. Life keeps moving forward.

My workdays are spent behind my closed office door. On any given day, we are about four here on-site. Nonetheless, team meetings happen by phone—we at the office dial in, just like our colleagues working remotely. My texts are filled with words like *precautions, triage, aerosols, hand hygiene, double-bagged, protective eyewear,* and *airborne droplets.* My hours are spent updating clinical procedures, patient transfer policies, HR communiqués on overtime pay, and recruiting efforts. Or working with colleagues to create posters explaining the what and the why and the how of it all to children, to seniors, to anyone who needs to know.

Words matter. I have always believed that. I have built a career around that. And yet, I never imagined that, in the midst of a global pandemic, I would officially be deemed an essential service. I am not on the front lines (and I remain in awe of those who are and what they are doing). I am heartened to know that maintaining the flow of quality, up-to-date information remains important.

I don't know when it will end. I can't guess what our next "normal" will look like.

I do believe it will be all right. Not the same. But all right.

Stay home if you can. Be careful if you can't.

Do remember that we are all in this together. Even when we're two metres apart. Don't let that bit of distance stop you from caring, loving, helping, and contributing. We are all building our next "normal" right now. We are creating what comes next in big ways and almost imperceptible ones, through the choices we make and why we make them. Let's make "what comes next" better.

COVID, Cruiser Cars, the Moon, and Me

DENISE DUGUAY

· · · · · ● · · · ·

I am standing in the semi-darkness of a little-used back trail that swings wide of the lookout on Mount Royal to maintain self-distancing. I have forgotten my mask, but that's not why I am in a fit of pique. I've just read that I face a $1,000 fine if I'm found walking with anyone, even six feet apart, with whom I don't live. So another month at least of COVID-19 quarantining, and not even a walk with a friend. The night's full moon—Pink Super Moon!—rises over the gloriously-named Belvédère Kondiaronk, looking south over the city.

I left on my evening walk like a child in a temper, planning to snub the Mountain and the inevitable full-moon crowd. I stomped through the wending streets of Atwater and The Boulevard, past austere stone houses set far back from empty streets, stingy lights showing brassy through the windows. Lost in my grumpy twists and turns, I found myself at the foot of a path, unfamiliar but—beckoning.

My feet made the decision. I wasn't quite on board with the plan, when the ring-road of Chemin Olmstead emerged from the bushes, blocked by a police cruiser. A runner, no mask, sensibly skirted the car. My feet directed themselves likewise, but my breath and heart, still feeling the climb, surged crazily.

"Slam the hood!" my arm was saying. "Slap the windshield! Scream in their faces!"

Shaken loose by shock, my mind hovered over the scene, gripped with a lizard-like need for... SOMEthing. But time ticked, and another walker passed and the metronome of my hips and legs—somehow still moving steadily—demurred, giving a wide berth to the vehicle and the constables inside (who hadn't even registered my threat).

As I neared the lookout, dusk was falling fast, the moon rising. I swiped open my phone to photograph the skyline and—there it was, another cruiser.

So here I am, framed by glowing red tail lights, where the rainbow ice-cream truck should have stood. A young guy steps toward the cruiser, angles his shoulder into the open driver's window, swaggers back. Accepting his challenge, I lunge. "Do it," a voice in my head commands, as my heart races back up to full speed. "Say it! Make SOMEthing happen." Again, my feet disobey, slowing enough that, as I step onto the lookout, the guy laughs easily, walks on. When I pass the constable, he smiles, looks tired. The moon is a cartoonishly big spotlight, paying us no mind. Across the lookout, the Peel Stairs are closed. Instead of rage, I feel quiet, safe. Held. The only way home is to retrace my steps. My feet know the way.

Walking It Off

JONATHAN KAPLANSKY

. . . .

The day begins as any other. I can see from the light through the blind that it must be going on 7 am. The sun is shining, which augurs a good day for me.

Meditation, exercises, music, coffee.

Open computer. Check email. Facebook. I ensure there are no work priorities, even though they often come in unexpectedly, and I have to answer right away that I'll take the job, usually responding within the hour.

I check the hourly forecast and decide that my walk to the summit should take place around 10 am. I go straight up to the top of Westmount, from Sherbrooke Street; I can make it in twenty minutes. No Fitbit needed, just a Swatch. Once I'm up there, I can take one of many routes. My goal is to walk sixty to ninety minutes.

Walking is inspiring. On cold days, I keep moving. Partway up the hill, I don't feel the chill. About half the time, I meet people I know and we chat while socially distanced—some dog walkers, some cyclists, some joggers, some other walkers. I have counted seven routes to the summit, and, once I'm up there, find endless variations, many involving ventures into the woods.

Coming back, there's a translation waiting. And the news. I limit the COVID-19 news. Basically, it is down to *The National* at 10 pm, and I don't give it the whole hour; I watch for thirty to forty minutes, and then it's time for bed. I get invitations from friends to which I'll respond: cooking projects and Zoom cocktail parties (I'll have my Egyptian Licorice tea), or coffee parties with folks from my swim team. People are phoning more, and if I phone them, I am more likely to find them at home or available. Long calls, short ones, but no marathons. Catching up with folks in Victoria, Hamilton, Ottawa. Not so much the States, because they just don't get it: "Canada is so strict!" "I'm glad the protesters have guns!" I avoid these topics, but these attitudes permeate the conversation nevertheless. It is hard to believe I spent seven years living there, so long ago.

I look up recipes I haven't made in years, complicated ones that will take more time but yield satisfying results. I contact someone I went to university with and haven't seen in twenty-seven years; I write that I thought about her today, making her falafel recipe, which I copied down in class. She replies: "*Merci de penser à moi, même en faisant des falafels!*"

By now I know people who are more fearful, who find it hard to leave their homes. Some still shop in stores; some are bored and restless. Still others have found a freedom in confinement. They are telling me that deconfinement may be difficult.

I understand.

Fear, Calm, and Nike VaporMax

ROBERT EDISON SANDIFORD

. . . .

How does a culture withstand the onslaught of a
pandemic? We survive first of all with the presence
of culture within us. It is to our inner culture that
we turn, the culture we carry in us through years of
unconscious osmosis and conscious acquisition.
—Ben Okri

My thirteen-year-old daughter Aeryn is afraid to die. On some days, it's a more abstract fear about the thought of not being here, of being nothing, an unfathomable void; on other days—like today—it's COVID-19.

"What if I catch it?" she asks.

"No one wants to catch it," I say.

It doesn't matter that she's less likely to die from it than, say, those over fifty like me, or those with pre-existing health conditions. "Fear accompanies the possibility of death," to quote from one of my favourite sci-fi shows, *FarScape*. "Calm shepherds its certainty."

Calm. How to get back there from here, and stay there?

Barbados (where we live) has reported its first two cases of COVID-19. Prime Minister Mia Mottley has said we can expect several more with increased testing.

When the world is too much with us, and we've played Uno for as long as we can, and we've binge-watched Game Show Network, with Steve Harvey family feuding, "Go read," I tell Aeryn.

She picks her copy of *Harriet's Daughter* by Marlene NourbeSe Philip from the kitchen table, heads for the living-room couch.

The YA novel is the latest title on her list to read. Not the school's—the system has yet to catch up with what's on offer to Caribbean students. The book seems to settle her. The world slows down just a microsecond—or three—while she quietly turns the pages.

These last few days, my mind has often gone back to when I was her age, and the US and USSR seemed poised to trigger World War Three.

"There was this movie," I say, sitting beside her. "*The Day After*. It captured our fears of nuclear cataclysm perfectly for the time." She's far too young to know about Jason Robards, who played the lead, so I explain.

Aside from reading, we tell stories. Or look at old photos of her mother and us together when the house was less cluttered, the paint fresher—more stories. Or read to each other from our cellphones. Much of that online literature is related to COVID-19, but not all. We talk.

Is there any other remedy for our present situation? All this talking—sharing—of fears and doubts, of hopes and dreams for a time after this.

"*Now* when am I going to wear my Nike VaporMax?" Her words are a teen's lament. We're leaving the house for what will be her last day of school.

I don't know how to answer. The shoes were to debut at our annual secondary school sporting showcase, until the Minister of Health and Wellness cancelled the last two days, and all such gatherings of over one hundred people.

"Another event," I suggest.

"But that won't be for a long time."

I stop to consider that that's possibly true.

"But there will be another event, at some point." She can't deny that either.

The thought may not entirely bring comfort, but it reminds us to care. It should remind us to hope for a time that's normal just beyond our reach—for the next day.

And for the next one after that.

An Uneasy Siesta

CONNIE GUZZO-MCPARLAND

. . . .

As controversy over the severity of COVID-19 dominated the airwaves, I felt a sense of relief when the Quebec premier finally took decisive action and announced a lockdown. We'd all take a collective pause and play it safe, while cocooning in our virus-free homes. I must confess, for a fleeting moment I experienced the same pleasure I'd had as a student, and then as a teacher, when the school board announced a snow day. Unexpectedly, a present fell from the heavens: the chance to snuggle up in bed, catch up on assignments, read, or simply laze around.

The sobering news of increasing infections in the province that followed soon made me realize how infantile that initial pleasure had been. This would not be a worry-free siesta!

Still, I resolved to make the most of it: I'd resume working on that non-fiction project; I'd declutter my clothes closets and home office; I might even tackle sorting the boxes of photos that take up precious real estate space in my cabinets—all this, while following a daily exercise routine and meal plan. I even bought two barbells at Canadian Tire before they sold out.

Working from home as a publisher didn't pose any restrictions. My team has done it for ten years. We cancelled physical launches and readings, but the more tedious clerical chores of running a publishing house remained.

I set out with a well-thought-out plan. A month later, self-isolation has dictated its own agenda:

I wake up early, have breakfast, and work on my writing project until email notifications pop up on my laptop, and I lose focus. After a shower, the TV beckons: I can't miss Justin Trudeau's daily briefings! CTV local news follows with reports of the daily toll of infections and deaths in Montreal nursing homes. While having my salad, I tune in to the Italian News on RAI TV for the European perspective, with more heartbreaking news of understaffed hospitals and seniors dying without a proper burial. I switch to CNN next for American breaking news, only to be provoked by the wacky statements of their president. The above-mentioned chores take up most of the afternoon with the newly-discovered technology of Zoom imposing virtual meetings at all hours of the day. A daily short, brisk walk is a must to stretch my limbs and clear my fogged-up mind, followed by a thankfully cheerful FaceTime interlude with my grandchildren, whom I haven't hugged in weeks. As I sit for another round of news, two barbells look at me wistfully from my sofa, but my walk should count for something. I cook dinner without counting micronutrients at this hour of the day. Reluctantly, I make a valiant attempt at decluttering. The eleven o'clock news repeats much of what I've heard throughout the day, but I still watch.

After a month, I have advanced, somewhat, on my writing project, but have barely finished organizing my desk drawer files and have yet to touch the photos. Plastic bags of unwanted clothes litter my bedroom floor, since the donation centres are closed. The exercise routine and meal plan? Well….

Ambivalence is slowly creeping in. Aside from fear of sickness, death, and the decreasing worth of my RRSPs, I wonder if this dubious gift of self-isolation will produce writing worthy of the gravitas and significance of the times, preoccupied as I am with the news and the trivial occupations of life–not to speak of the Zoom meetings. Yet, is it not precisely those banal daily routines that this virus has stolen from so many, and that thousands on ICU respirators are struggling to regain?

PENNING THE PANDEMIC
The View From My Living Room

ARIELA FREEDMAN

. . . .

The term "living room" came into common use after the First World War. Before the living room, there was the front parlour. This room was a formal showpiece, and before the proliferation of funeral homes, parlours were used to lay out the dead. After the many deaths of the First World War and the Spanish Flu, the front parlour became a haunted space. As early as 1910, the Dutch-born editor of *Ladies' Home Journal* had already published an article titled, "A Living Room is Born," suggesting it was time to revive the staid front parlour—that is, it was time for the room to come back to life. The living room was a rebranding of a space where the dead were once venerated, at a time when there were so many that the house could no longer hold them.

As we have retreated into our homes, with the goal of minimizing the numbers of the dead, I have seen more living rooms in this period than in my entire life. I have seen the living rooms of friends and strangers, of my students and my colleagues, of celebrities and politicians. They are not all living rooms, as such—they are kitchens and bedrooms and gardens, private spaces now casually on display.

I have seen more living rooms in this past week than in my entire life.

Some of the revelations are surprising. Arnold Schwarzenegger has a country-cozy kitchen. The walls are painted sage green and cream, and the shelves behind the table are crowded with photos and bric-a-brac. His quarantine videos star his mini donkey Lulu, his pony Whiskey, and his dog Cherry. He feeds them carrots by hand inside the house. Lady Gaga lets her three slobbery bulldogs lie on her grey velvet couch. I guess the wall behind her is marble, but it looks like lavatory tile. She could probably clean her windows, and she is wearing sunglasses indoors and at night. Taylor Swift's cat bed looks like a modern sculpture, a copper globe inside the skeleton of a steel cube. Jimmy Fallon has a tubular slide that takes him from floor to floor. One of the Alvin Ailey dancers has dyed her white puppy's ears and tail hot pink. So many people have fairy lights and, like me, too much paper pinned to their fridge.

Magazines and social media have long showcased the interiors of celebrity homes as a way of providing the illusion of access and intimacy. Still, there is something more vulnerable in this new display, without the stagers, without the camera crew or even the cleaners. There is lint on Cardi B's rug. During an Indigo Girls living room livestream, someone asks about the water damage on the ceiling. We know the real colours of everybody's hair.

At times, the performance of social responsibility grates against the reminder of social inequality. When Arnold lectures those on spring break while smoking a cigar in his hot tub, it is hard not to think that if everyone had a mansion, a hot tub, and a California garden, it would be no great hardship to stay home.

I am in my living room at the moment, sitting on the first couch I ever bought. I can see the park across the street from my window. It is empty. My husband is working in the basement, and my children are in their bedrooms listening to online classes. I can picture them in the different levels of the house, like in a Richard Scarry illustration where the wall is lifted out so you can see the people inside. My husband has started seeds in the basement, and, while I question the wisdom of using chicken manure as indoor fertilizer when we are stuck at home, I am excited to see the plants begin to sprout. I know we are lucky to have this living space and to have a garden for when the sidewalks become forbidden, but I am restless by nature.

"Can we talk about what we do afterwards?" I ask my son, thinking of restaurants and the companionate orgy of a Montreal summer.

He says, Nope, not yet. But when? "Teach me to care and not to care," T.S. Eliot writes in "Ash Wednesday." "Teach me to sit still."

Just sit on your couch, they say. Never has so little been asked of so many by so many. Nonetheless, it is hard to sit still. It is hard to let go when you don't know what's really gone. It is hard to live in a state of anticipatory grief. It is hard to imagine what we will see when this is finally over, when we leave our living rooms, and close the door, and walk the streets, and meet what's left.

Touch and Go

DEBORAH OSTROVSKY

· · · · · ● ● ● ● ·

I go out for a walk, and my legs start to shake. I'm dizzy, confused. By evening, I have a fever. It breaks at 5:58 am. I develop a dry cough, shortness of breath, and more night fevers. My husband takes me to the mobile clinic in the Quartier des Spectacles to get swabbed for COVID-19. Five days later, when I finally receive my negative test result, I'm already on my way to the ER, where a triage nurse is so anxious that she jolts backward every time I cough, calling an orderly to wheel me to a "COVID bed."

I receive IV fluids for dehydration, another swab, x-rays, and care from nurses and doctors who display a preternatural combination of compassion and trepidation. They hesitate before touching me. But their jobs require them precisely to touch me, palpate me, insert needles in my veins, and place EKG sensors on my chest and legs. Between fits of coughing, I focus on their eyes: blue, dark brown, hazel. *Are you as scared of my body and its infectious potential as much as I am of yours?* I think to myself as a nurse draws blood from my arm and administers IV antibiotics. The staff come and go from my room, faces covered with masks, goggles, and shields. They circle my bed, creating a halo of distance between us.

"How are you coping?" I ask them on my second night in hospital, a sincere but awkward attempt at creating a connection. "It's really tough," says the technician who took my CT scan for a suspected pulmonary embolism. He gestures for permission to put his gloved hand on mine. Then, he pulls away as a chatty orderly wheels me back to my room. Somewhere in the hallway, I hear an altercation, as security escorts a woman outside. She has refused to leave her spouse, who is being whisked off to ICU. At the nursing station, a staff member tells her colleagues that, if she falls ill, she wants them to know she loves them.

Three COVID-19 tests later, I'm still negative. The diagnosis: bacterial pneumonia. No need for oxygen. Just rest, fluids, antibiotics. The attending physician explains that cases this severe usually require a few days in hospital. But the risk of coronavirus exposure is too high. Better to get out of here, he says.

Today, bedridden and still coughing, I think about the last time I walked outside, at the mobile testing clinic. I moved along the length of the big, white screening tent along Rue Jeanne-Mance—the street named after a French nurse. I stopped to scan the façade of the *Musée d'art contemporain de Montréal* to the east, high above the crowd, all of us lined up, clutching our health cards, waiting to get swabbed. I thought of Lot's wife as I looked back, trying to remember all the faces in line behind me. I'm still unsure why I did that, and what I was hoping to see.

When the Teddy Takes Notes

CURTIS MCRAE

· · · · · · · · ·

I was kicked out of my apartment a few days before the pandemic shut down the world. Standing on the corner of my street with a single foldable box, I pulled out my cellphone and dialled home. Later, I lay on my mother's couch, across the room from my younger sister's human-sized teddy bear. I couldn't speak with my therapist, unless it was by teleconference, to which I had an aversion. I tried to figure out why with the bear, my new therapist. I hadn't had any breakthroughs. The bear nodded and took notes.

"In my dream," I mused, "a man clad in loose, black clothes broke into my home and tied my family to our kitchen chairs with thick rope. He dragged the chairs into the living room, me beside my sister, my sister beside my mother, my mother beside me. He asked me where my father was. I told him that he had left. The man began to laugh."

I heard a chuckle from across the room. When I looked over, the stuffed bear was covering part of its face. I glared into its marble eyes. It understood the warning. I carried on.

"He pulled a speaker from his backpack, plugged the auxiliary cord into his iPod, and blared 'We Are Family' by Sister Sledge into the stillness of the night. He danced around the room and laughed hysterically. I wiggled my toes. My mother tapped her foot. It was all very nice."

I yawned and looked over to make sure it was listening.

"I returned to waking life and heard Sister Sledge fading out, until I was in my empty, quiet room—as I had been before I fell asleep, as I would continue to be, until my sister knocked on my door at 9 am, asking if I wanted something from Starbucks. I nodded my head. She closed the door. It was all very nice. We are family, you know."

The teddy bear continued taking notes. I looked at the walls of my childhood home.

"I know you practise CBT, but, in your opinion, is that worth analyzing?"

There was no answer. I was lying on my mother's couch, speaking to my sister's teddy bear. It was the only quiet I would have all day. My mother was shopping at Costco for our weekly groceries, my sister on an unnecessary coffee run.

My phone vibrated in my pocket. It was my father, whose new girlfriend is a nurse. I ignored the call, because I was immune-compromised and because he probably wanted to go for a walk.

"What about my father?"

Still nothing. A still room. A kitchen chair. The hummingbirds outside.

"I suppose you're right; it's who was there."

The bear leaned into the room.

"Can I be fortunate and still be self-pitying?"

It looked into a corner of the room, avoiding any eye contact.

"Yeah, I guess you're right."

The room was quiet. I heard the garage door open.

"Well, what do I owe you for this session?"

The bear remained silent. The garage door slammed shut. The day carried on.

"That much, huh?"

ÇA VA BIEN ALLER

KENNETH RADU

· · · · · ● · · ·

Ça va?
My neighbours across the road display a rainbow with the words *ÇA VA BIEN ALLER* painted in garish colours. It's like a form of Facebook cheerfulness, I think, to post your optimism for passing pedestrians to see. Well, not pedestrians, as no one passes these days, except the odd, relentless cyclist. A car coincidentally drove by, which reminded me of my stroll to the village the other day: there were no other pedestrians, the town devoid of street traffic and people, like an episode of *The Twilight Zone*. I noticed at the local station that the price of gas has fallen to seventy-two cents a litre. Great, but I'm not driving anywhere, and I still have a nearly full tank of gas to take me to the *marché* in another town every ten days or so. With any luck... I am hopeful... it will last me for the duration of the pandemic, at the end of which I'm sure gas prices will soar once again.

If I putter about the garden and my neighbours across the road notice, they wave and I return the greeting. Réjean, who lives next door, stops on his side of the bushes and begins a conversation in French, at least two metres between us; half his words are picked up and muffled by the ceaseless wind. I am also going deaf but never wear my hearing aids outside. The wind blows, making the aids whistle inside my skull, thereby making it impossible to hear anything at all. So I shout back in answer to what, judging by the lift in Réjean's voice at the end, is a question: "*ÇA VA BIEN ALLER!*" It's a serviceable phrase, since it not only signals happy expectations, but is also a fitting end to a friendly exchange over scraggly spirea bushes. It's time for the annual check up of the devices, but my audio-prosthetist phoned yesterday to cancel the appointment.

This and other cancellations unsettle my nerves, as much as anxiety about infection. Appointments of one kind or another are a feature of my days, as they must be for many people. Remove them, and I feel abandoned in a kind of limbo of altered circumstances, where nothing can be promised except that one day—that fabulous day when contagion has ceased and crowds appear on the streets once again—we'll pick up where we left off. Réjean waves good-bye, which is a relief, because shouting in the breeze creates its own kind of stress.

With writing and reading to do—those essential, uncancelled events of my days, I enter the house and wash my hands, although I've touched nothing outside, neither the soil nor the post delivered by Gaston *le facteur* to the roadside mail box. He shouted out his car window: "*Salut, monsieur Radu, ça va?*" I smiled and shouted back: "*ÇA VA BIEN ALLER!*"

From My Window—Some COVID Views

WENDY REICHENTAL

. . . .

Like everyone in this COVID-19 pandemic, I have completely lost a
sense of time. I have done my best to keep to a new type of schedule and to be cognizant of what month and day of the week it is, and
where we are on the spectrum of time; but being in a zombie-like
state of disbelief can at times make you lose track of it all. Somewhere
during these past few weeks, I noticed another strange phenomenon
to add to my growing list of new habits: I have morphed into the
iconic character Gladys Kravitz, the peering-behind-her-window-
curtain, nosy neighbour across the street from Samantha Stephens,
our favourite witch on a broom from the classic TV show, *Bewitched.*

My standard living-room window has suddenly become my new
guilty pleasure, replacing Netflix with real-time laughs and drama.
Here, every day safely distancing behind my pane of glass, I find
myself drawn to the comings and goings of people and their new
routines during this strange *Twilight Zone* time we are living in.
Today at 10:15 am, I look forward to seeing this interesting older
couple—a gentleman sporting a stylish houndstooth cap and wooden
cane, and his female companion, partner, or spouse—who will be out
for their morning stroll. I have never noticed this couple before in
my neighbourhood, but lately my block has become a thoroughfare
for walkers, cyclists, skate boarders, and joggers. The lunch hour
has become a particularly busy time slot, when dog walkers and
families alike come out together but remain apart to greet the warm
afternoon sun and take in some fresh air.

I watch as my street has suddenly become this hub of activity and
remember the B.C. times (Before COVID-19), when we might have

taken for granted picayune choices, such as double kissing, or being able to shake a hand, or offering the tightest of hugs to our loved ones. In true Gladys form, I call out to my lately rounder husband to get up from the couch and come quickly over to our window, to see the strange behaviours of our various neighbours across the street on their driveways where they are having conversations using handheld loudspeakers. At another corner, I notice what appears to be grandparents waving to their toddler grandchildren from their windows. We are both witnessing what has become the new norm—drive-by visitations.

All this observing is making me look inward, at me and my life, and making me so grateful for what I have: my health, my family, and even my Abner-Kravitz-like, occasionally-cantankerous, nap-loving husband. But don't get me wrong: I also can't wait to leave this house and be 'socially distancing' myself from my living room window, remembering this dark time with a renewed conviction about cherishing all the mundane nuances in our lives.

The Daughter Returns

SU J SOKOL

• • • • • • • •

Today, my twenty-eight-year-old daughter moved back in with me. She brought a Chromebook, an eight-pack of toilet paper, a coffee grinder, two beers, a bottle of wine, her roller blades, and a colouring book entitled *Fleurs antistress à colorier*.

When Mara moved out at age seventeen, I never expected her to return, even for a temporary, indefinite period. Fiercely independent, she had been practising her flight from the family nest for most of her childhood. This was the kid who'd begged to go to a slumber party at age three, who'd gone to sleep-away camp at nine, and who'd had a steady job since she was fourteen. Yet, despite my pride in her independence, I couldn't help wondering if we'd done something to drive her out.

The morning of April 1, I was participating in a Zoom meeting when the mattress arrived. I quickly put myself on mute and dragged it into the house. The week before, Mara had told us she'd like to move in temporarily for the company, and also, just in case—I have respiratory issues, and she worries. Still, her childhood bed was very uncomfortable, so we found a soft cotton, made-in-Canada mattress on sale and ordered it right away, despite our usual hesitation to make spontaneous online purchases.

With Mara's arrival, more new routines developed. I'm doing my regular job from home, using the tiny half-room behind the kitchen, where I work on files and offer phone assistance to people who'd normally come in person to our social rights clinic. Mara's father, Glenn, still cycles to the organization where he is employed, or works at home in the cluttered office upstairs. Mara, a high school math

160

teacher at a school for kids with learning disabilities, claimed the living room to tutor, prepare materials for her students, help her colleagues, and take an online calculus class.

At night, we try to relax. We read, talk to friends and family on the phone (Glenn), attend Zoom writing-group meetings (me), play online poker with friends (Mara). Sometimes, all three of us will play a board game together. That first night, Mara played Scrabble with us and won, despite her boycott of the game ever since her little brother began soundly beating her. (She couldn't have known he'd eventually become a top-ranked tournament Scrabble player.)

The other night, we were talking about the future. Mara, who doesn't currently have a partner, spoke about the possibility of moving back into the house one day, if she ends up having kids on her own. We could even help raise them. I reacted with pleased surprise. Maybe we hadn't inadvertently pushed her away after all. Or at least, not too far away. I felt grateful and humbled. How fortunate it is to have children, strong and independent, who also understand the meaning of social solidarity.

Sneering at the Snark

BRIAN CAMPBELL

. . . .

There is this poster that is conspicuously placed on a papered-over storefront on Bernard Avenue, in my neighbourhood of Mile End—it's like a voice echoing from what seems a distant past, a perpetual sneering at the snark, at the presumptions of cool. The poster's been here a few months. To have lasted that long, it obviously must have been respected by others who had also posted there about cultural events.... Remember those?

The street's so empty, it's surreal. The late afternoon is normally rush hour, but, today, there's virtually no traffic. The restaurants and boutiques are shuttered, with signs on their doors: "*Fermé, jusqu'à nouvel ordre*" or "*jusqu'a... ?*" A few pedestrians, some wearing facemasks, cast long shadows as they cross the street. I proceed to the local *fruiterie* where, for our groceries, I'll risk my life again.

In the enforced quietude, my brain is a busy mishmash of memes and quotations from a torrent of online articles shared on Facebook or Twitter. Fran Leibowitz in *The New Yorker*: "It is a very startling thing to be my age—I'm sixty-nine—and to have something happen that doesn't remind you of anything else." Paul Krugman in *The New York Times*: "We're in the economic equivalent of a medically-induced coma." But then, from Mr. Very Stable Genius, there's this: "A lot of people will have this and it is very mild... so you know, we have thousands, or hundreds of thousands of people that get better, just by, you know, sitting around and even going to work." That was March 2. Today, he accused the World Health Organization of "severely mismanaging and covering up the spread of the coronavirus."

A sign from the present resonates with me more deeply than that bloviating voice or these fading advertisements: a painted rainbow, with the phrase *Ça va bien aller.* There are at least a dozen of these in windows on my street. Most are painted by children. *It's going to be fine.* On a deeper level, *This too will pass.* And deeper still, *We're all in this together.*

It's stunning, what we've given up: visits, events, cafés, restaurants, workouts at the Y, kisses, handshakes. One meme: *We stand apart to stand together.* Another: *We are being given the opportunity to stitch a new garment—one that fits all humanity and nature.*

I count myself fortunate. My wife and I get along, we live in decent accommodations, and, as artists, we have no shortage of things to do in our comparatively splendid isolation. There have been synthetic, but very real encounters on Zoom and Skype, and a virtual launch of my CD on Facebook, because the real launch was cancelled.

My day ends with coronavirus death counts; at this moment, 487 in Quebec, over a thousand in Canada, 136,000 around the world. Like many, I have seen my sleep affected. My focus too. A cloud of low-grade depression is to be warded away, a suffocating "meh."

Great things have been made of *meh*: the poetry of Larkin, the novels of Don DeLillo. I feel this *meh* gathering into a poem, a song—at the very least, this article.

As I write, a sore throat—it's come and gone over the last few days—makes me uneasy. Maybe *meh* is to be treasured.

Nothing. *Nada. Rien du tout.*

GREGORY MCKENZIE

· · · · · • • • ·

N othing. That's just about all I have to do today. Nothing. *Nada. Rien du tout.*

Maybe stare at the brick wall outside the bedroom window. Look at the trees that peek out over the top of the building next door. If I'm lucky, I might see a squirrel. Or a bird or two. Crows, mostly. And if I'm really lucky, I might glimpse a plane. Then I can wonder where it's headed. Pass a little more time staring at the sky. Surely there are no passengers. Nowhere to go. These planes must carry only packages where the passengers might have been—packages heading some place where other people are stuck inside, staring at their brick walls and the sky, just like me.

It should be easy for me. I was pretty much a shut-in already. Might spend my days pretending to translate. Or maybe I'd go out to the grocery store a couple of times a week and complain about it. Or I might see a friend every now and again. Now there's no reason to go out at all. We buy groceries in bulk, so we don't have to go out. We only talk on the phone, so we don't physically have to have contact with our friends. So, now I really am a shut-in.

I could go for a walk. But somehow that seems like I'd be breaking a rule. I might be coughed or sneezed on. Or worse: somehow spread the virus that I surely don't have to elderly, sick neighbours whom I've never seen on my block before. So maybe I'll just stay in bed and stare at the wall a bit more. And wallow in self-pity... because that's just about all there is to do today.

But I'm lucky, really, because I'm not alone. There's Carl, my boyfriend, and the cats. The cats make me laugh. And the darkness and grey days usually let up, and it doesn't always rain. Today, the sun even streamed in through the window, as I stared at the wall outside. And I have Netflix, and a computer, and toilet paper. And enough food to eat for a couple of weeks. And I have Portuguese lessons by Skype and a writing workshop by Zoom. But dammit, I miss those runs to the grocery I used to complain about so much. I miss not having to buy in bulk. And I really miss seeing those friends who I used to see only occasionally.

Today's April 15. But really, it could be yesterday or tomorrow, because right now days are pretty much all the same.

Solitude Has not Been a Sorrowtude

ROKSANA BAHRAMITASH

. . . .

Don't feel lonely
The entire universe is inside you.
—Rumi

Part of my life was lived in a culture in which the passing of a loved one called for forty days of mourning. In the midst of a global pandemic, I am well into my fourth week of self-isolation. Sad as it has been to witness the loss of many lives and the possibility of losing one's own, a sense of surrender, content, inspiration, and something like euphoria has surfaced. I'm not sure why.

As the world around me shut down, an inner voice took over and a journey began, one that has brought me closer to my cultural heritage. Indeed, the word "quarantine" comes from *al-Arba'iniya* to mean forty days in isolation, coined by a Persian—Ibn Sina, known in the West as Avicenna and a father of early modern medicine (980-1037). He was the first to understand that to prevent the spread of contagious diseases such as cholera, people should be isolated for forty days—an idea that then travelled to Italy, where the term "quarantine" entered the Western lexicon.

My first few days of self-isolation were consumed by the shock of a global pandemic and the innate desire to control the future. But soon, my normal self resurfaced: I was grateful for the time I have on this planet. Every single day is a gift—a bonus. It was not so long ago that I had a rendezvous with death; I barely survived two severe brain tumours.

In quarantine, I sought salvation by delving into the wisdom of Persian mystical poetry. Rumi, Hafiz, and Attar rooted me, nourished my soul, and shed light on my deepest love—writing. Ah, yes, my unpublished book, a memoir: it was funded by the Canada Council for the Arts, and, at one time, in the hands of a top New York agent who loved it but was unable to find a publisher. In that particular year, too many biographies by Iranian women had already been published. What once seemed like bad news made me secretly happy, because I knew I could do better.

Yet, the opportunity didn't come—until now. The pandemic has been a time to listen, to observe, to be curious, and to be contemplative. It has given me a sense of elation. The dark madness of the world outside has brought a shimmering light of inner wisdom, the serenity to listen to the writer inside me, a cherished love that was always close to my heart.

Heeeere's Pat!

STEPHANIE MOLL

. . . .

Back in early March, after the biggest snowfall of the season, my husband David and I were out walking when I had a profound revelation: I had never built a snowman (or snow-person, I should say). I should explain that I'm a native Texan, a permanent resident of Montreal for only the past two years. So, I became excited about the possibility of building a snow-person—only to have my hopes dashed, as David announced that it was not the "right kind." Apparently, this snow was too powdery and would not hold. Seriously? Who even knew that was a "thing"? Certainly not this newbie!

Then, as luck would have it, shortly after everything started closing down, we had another little snowfall on March 17, for several hours and... insert drum roll here—it was the "right" kind of snow. Yay! I rushed to the kitchen for supplies, only to discover we were out of carrots and coal. Fortunately, we had radishes, a large banana pepper, and some coins. So, we bundled up and headed to the small park next door, because I was told we needed enough space to "roll the balls." Whatever that meant. Silly me: I thought you just mushed a bunch of snow together. David helpfully instructed me about the correct system for building the said snow-person—his tormented years in Massachusetts finally paid off big time.

We had so much fun! We were the only people in the park, so it was totally safe, and it was a welcome relief from being inside.

In these days of self-isolation/social distancing/sheltering in place, or whatever you want to call it, I miss my workout classes at the YMCA, my weekly mah-jong game, and all the other activities

I usually enjoy. I am incredibly grateful for the wonderful ways that technology has enabled me to stay connected during these crazy times.

I'm looking forward to a walk outside again today. The sun is peeking out and the temperatures are supposed to rise above 1°C. Anything at or above freezing feels warm-ish these days, but I admit I am eager for spring to arrive!

Virtual hugs to everyone. Please stay safe out there!

Scheduling the Days

HARRY RAJCHGOT

． ． ． ． ● ● ● ． ．

Despite a string of cold, windy, and sometimes rainy days, no matter the weather, I've left the house every day—a fairly solitary activity, until today. Today was one of the few bright, shiny days in a while: sunny, with little wind. I went for a walk. In the before-COVID-19 era—B.C.—a warm spring day was a gift. Today, I cringed, knowing many others would be out, tired of being cooped up in their homes.

Côte-Saint-Luc, where I live, used to boast many walking places, long wide streets, and plenty of parks.

Playground equipment has been closed off with wire fence barriers. Most strollers honour the suggested two-metre gap between us, but larger families fill the sidewalk, spilling onto the road. To avoid them, I walk in the middle of the road. I nervously scan behind me for cars or buses, navigating around elderly walkers moving forward slowly and young children looping around on their bicycles, under the watchful eye of a parent. Adult cyclists glide by, invading "social" distances. I wince, hoping for the best. I see a first robin. Hope.

Then I see a shiny dime on the sidewalk. Should I pick it up? I read silver and copper kill viruses. Is it true? I can't resist. I bend, scoop it up, and slip it into my pocket. The regrets begin. Stupid me. What if...?

I focus on the fact that that my hand doesn't touch anything. When I finally get home, unnerved, I slip the key in the lock and, using my other hand, turn, push the door handle, enter, close the door with the elbow I haven't sneezed into, and go directly to wash my hands: soap, twenty seconds, dry well, dig into my pocket, retrieve the dime, place it on newspaper, spray hand with disinfectant, wash the dime with water, drop it into my spare change bin, relieved. Again, I wash my hands. Strip off my winter jacket, strip off my jeans, and drop them in the washer. Think, think, think. Never break the chain of infection. Think, think, think. Fresh jeans. Sit down, stop thinking. Call my brother, a paediatrician living in Toronto.

He feels he has to continue serving his patients. Vaccines on schedule. Newborns evaluated. Routine exams by FaceTime or Zoom. He fears he'll need to wear plastic garbage bags when the supply of gowns runs low. Masks and gloves are running out. He jumps back when one child suddenly sneezes. He changes his shirt for each patient. When he gets home, he undresses in the garage, drops clothing in the washing machine, sets it to high. His son, training in pneumonology, works at an Ottawa hospital. His mother worries constantly about both.

I retired from dental practice in December, at the Children's Hospital, before this chaos arrived. I'm grateful. I was seeing young patients too. Many had systemic diseases, immune disorders, heart or other problems. I'm seventy-three years old, diabetic, with a history of cardiac problems. I think, think, think.

I hope tomorrow's weather will be terrible.

Chronic City

KAREN ISABEL OCAÑA

· · · · · · · · ·

The days drag on. The story is the same. The story changes. The story is grim. But it's not altogether grim. The number of infected, the number of the dead climbs. More and more countries are under lockdown. But, in some places, they are loosening the restrictions. Some places have a plan—a detailed one. Others do not want to say, or do not know what to say.

A friend of mine is ill with COVID-19.

Today, the text arrives. She is going to make it. She has been moved out of intensive care. She has a room of her own, for recovery. As I write this, it's snowing, but it's sunny too. The sky is half-blue. The glass is half-full. You will be forgiven for thinking it's half full of disinfectant. Hope is a straw. You cling to it. But do not drink from it.

You call your mother, if you have one. The sound of her voice is uplifting. We call our children and their children. It's hectic. People are working from home. Home has become a workplace, or a hospital, and, for some, a prison. Home is still the best place, if you're lucky to have a place of your own. Or it's not. Home may not be the place you need to be—you may want to be in a hospital, you may need to be in an ICU. You are fortunate if you have choices. We are fortunate to be in Canada.

I call my friend, and she answers in a voice woozy with sleep and morphine. She sounds happy. I feel delirious. It's a blissful feeling to know she made it, to hear her voice. To connect after so many weeks of waiting. To speak and know we will talk to one another yet again. We do.

We cherish the moment. We try to do what is required. We help friends and family carry their burdens, and the people with whom we work. There's a shared burden and there's a shared foe. The science is emerging, but not keeping pace. The killer is several steps ahead. The chase is on. The target has been called at times a chimera, and, at others, sneaky. The chase has been called a war. But, really? Really, it's not.

We are not victims of a hoax. We know deep down. Deep down we know that the good times were too good to last. That there was a price to pay for all of the ridiculous ease with which we, we sneaky ones, glide through reality, virtually and actually. Landing here, there, everywhere. Treating the environment like a garbage dump. Call this a reality check. It will be okay, they say. We'll pick up the pieces of our broken world. There is a saying that the most beautiful objects are the ones that have been put back together. My friend is on the mend and my heart with her.

Spiders

NOAH ALLISON

· · · · · · · · ·

My main objective as a visiting scholar at McGill University during the 2019-2020 academic year was to complete my dissertation. Although I spent many years living in New York, my perspective, growing up in Southern California, was that Montreal's long winter would facilitate productive writing outcomes; for the most part, it did, even though it was cut short by the onslaught of the virus.

During my last two weeks in Montreal, tangible indicators of the contagion remained elusive. The only notions of its presence came in the form of red circles overlaid on a black-and-white rendering of the United States that is still displayed on the front page of *The New York Times*. In cities most affected by the virus's ravages, death and illness usually occur behind closed doors. While I conceptually understood the importance of being closer to family, the threats of pandemic conditions seemed so far away.

I left Montreal on March 26, 2020, and moved into a single-storey bungalow that sits behind a house built in 1907 in the Arlington Heights district in Central Los Angeles. Between the house and the bungalow, there is a relatively extensive garden that is seen as orderly by some and chaotic by others. Prior to my moving in, the one-bedroom bungalow that has two bathroom sinks, a large kitchen, and a skylight had been empty of humans for years. The day after I arrived from Montreal, I began setting up the space to make it comfortable for an indefinite period of time. There were spiders in more places than not. At first, I attempted to catch them in a glass jar and release them in the garden. Although they were only daddy longlegs, arachnophobia prevented me from getting close to some of the bigger ones. Did I feel guilty for displacing the spiders? No, not really. But I didn't want to kill them. Still, after spending forty-five minutes of carefully trying to remove all the spiders and webs from the bungalow, I thought my work was done—that is, until I went to wash my hands in one of the bathroom sinks only to have a couple dozen baby spiders run up the drain as I turned on the water. I yelped in surprise and leapt out of the bathroom. I irrationally ran to my toolbox, grabbed the can of RAID Ant & Roach Killer—remnants from my New York life—and began uncontrollably spraying the sink. The tiny little black dots immediately stopped moving.

I convinced myself that their untimely death was painless. Only a few kept fighting the poison. Since spiders likely do not contemplate "what it means to be," I figured that it does not matter to them when they are no longer "being." I repeat this to myself each time I grab the can of RAID after seeing a pholcidae, or anything that reminds me of one: dust, a poorly patched hole, or a pincher bug. Each day, it becomes a hunt and something to which I look forward. Under the toilet. Behind the bed. In the closet. Between the books. On the side of the couch. Above the mirror. On the candelabra. Always more and always somewhere new. While the past two weeks have been marked by calamitous pandemic conditions and mental insecurities stemming from dissertation writing, killing spiders has become one of the few tangible, attainable, and enjoyable activities filling my days.

Isolation and the Shadow of Death

TIMOTHY NIEDERMANN

. . . .

Strangely enough, the self-isolation inflicted on the rest of the world by the coronavirus pandemic hasn't affected me much. I was already isolated.

A few years ago, I was forced by circumstance to leave Montreal and return to my family home in the countryside. But my personal misfortune was a boon to my parents, who were then in their late eighties. Both soon developed serious health issues, so my presence became essential. They are at the moment in their mid-nineties. Their health is excellent, and, thankfully, their minds are still sharp. And they have me, which means no nursing home—they are able to stay in the house they have lived in for sixty years.

To care for elderly parents, however, even those in as good shape as mine, is to see your world contract. As time has passed, my parents' activity has lessened, and my responsibilities for them and the house have expanded. Their isolation—and mine—became a fact long ago. They spend most of the day reading, a routine punctuated only by meals and a long afternoon nap. I am chauffeur, errand boy, cook, and gardener, the latter being at times burdensome, as we have several hectares of land to maintain.

In essence, every day is the same, except for the weather and what I serve to eat. Since I have to be here to prepare every meal, a genuine social life has long been out of the question. My only respite has been my daily trip to the local gym, which closed due to the pandemic.

The relentless monotony of the routine tends to mask the fact that this is also a waiting game. One must forcibly stay alert for the next health crisis to appear—and prepare emotionally for the inevitable event that will signal the final downturn into oblivion. "Which one will go first?" is a thought that is never far off.

Nevertheless, death has been a relatively distant presence—a dark, looming cloud on the horizon, to be sure, but not a shadow on our doorstep. I have looked at it as a far-away observer might, aware that, at some future date, my role will be to call an ambulance yet again and maintain the security of routine for the one left behind.

The coronavirus has changed that, however slightly. My mother cannot go to her weekly hair appointment for the time being, but otherwise pretty much everything has remained the same. A health worker, these days usually masked and gloved, still comes in twice a week to bathe my mother, something made necessary by a fall that broke her femur eighteen months ago. I don a mask whenever I leave the house on errands.

But the spectre of death has come into closer view, and it has a name: COVID-19. My parents are in the age group most vulnerable to the virus. If either contracts it, likely both will quickly die. The house is big enough (I and my three siblings grew up in it), that I can practise a form of social distancing, only getting near my parents at meals.

Although limited, there is contact with the outside. I do the shopping on Thursday. The healthcare worker comes on Tuesday and Friday. Those are the dangerous days—the days of possible exposure. Otherwise, the routine goes on. But the shadow is much closer to our door.

Most people isolate to limit contact with possible carriers of the virus, because those carriers are anonymous. If death arrives at our house, however, we know who will usher it in: either the healthcare worker... or me.

PENNING THE PANDEMIC
Homeschooling

GREG SANTOS

· · · · · · · · · ·

"You're used to homeschooling your kids. What's your advice to other parents who are now in your shoes?"

In a Zoom meeting recently, I was asked this question by an acquaintance. Taken aback, I found myself struggling for a good answer. I said something incoherent about how it's different now during the global COVID-19 pandemic, but I couldn't properly articulate my thoughts, which left me frustrated. As I write this, I am still struggling to make sense of it all.

This isn't normal, even for us homeschoolers. Yes, we've had five years of experience homeschooling our children, but none of this is normal.

I find the word "homeschooling" to be problematic. My wife and I view the world as the kids' school. Although yes, academic work—French, science, history, geography, English, math, and so on—tends to take place at home, it is usually condensed into two or three hours per day. Until COVID-19, the kids had lots of time each day for outside activities. Home was where we started and ended each day, but we were never "stuck" at home for long periods of time. Until COVID-19, there were piano and swimming lessons to attend, forest school each week, Girl Guide and Scout meetings, acting classes, Sunday school, and so many playdates, playgrounds, and parks. There were field trips to museums, visits with the grandparents, and the list goes on. Our calendar, normally filled with activities, is instead filled with crossed-out plans. This void is the new normal.

Yes, we still keep up the "home" part of our homeschooling routine. It is a blessing that we can continue following the curriculum that my wife designed at the beginning of the year. That helps maintain a sense of normalcy for us.

But a sense of loss and grief also permeates our days. Whereas I would have been out many afternoons, teaching poetry, creative writing, and essay writing courses at different venues and institutions, I find myself housebound, with all remaining work shifted online. We often find ourselves claiming different corners of the house, attempting to do our own thing in peace, but sometimes we end up stepping on each other's toes. There is a large void in our daily lives. A cloud of anxiety hangs over us. When will this end?

At the same time, just as the kids' activities are cancelled (or, in most cases, moved to this new world called Zoom), we have noticed that they have a remarkable ability to keep themselves entertained and educated. They make up the most amazing imaginative games with their toys. They make treasure hunts, create board games. Our eldest wrote a chapter book. They are taking on more chores and clean up after themselves with less complaining than during the "pre-COVID" days. We are often in awe of their resilience and creativity.

Those are the good days. Of course, not all days are good. Other days, they argue and scream. But then they make up. We have learned to trust that our children will learn, even without a roster of outside activities.

As a writer, however, I find it challenging to write during this pandemic. Normally, I would put pen to paper, jot lines and notes on my phone, or type something on my laptop. I find myself doing that less and less.

My new book, *Ghost Face*, was supposed to launch this year at DC Books' Spring Launch, scheduled during the 2020 Blue Metropolis International Literary Festival on May 2. I had been eagerly awaiting the event. *Ghost Face* is my most personal book, and I had been working on it since 2008. But Blue Met was cancelled, including the launch for me and my fellow DC Books authors. I don't know when *Ghost Face* is going to be published. Most of my teaching contracts, planned readings, and the events that I was anticipating have been postponed or cancelled. Many of my writer and artist peers find themselves in similar positions.

So, *do* I have advice for others who are new to this housebound version of homeschooling? I would say: start slowly and start gently. Even for those of us who have homeschooled for years, it is difficult to adjust to the new psychological climate. Perhaps you could consider "homeschooling" as just spending time with your kids doing something you all enjoy. It's bound to be educational, but, more importantly, stress-relieving. You could dust off a board game. Get out the pencils and paper, and just draw together. Read a book out loud, or listen to a podcast together. And listen to what the kids have to say. Many times, their ideas are better than anything we could come up with. No matter what, be gentle with yourselves. Don't expect to be able to do what you would normally do (or what veteran homeschoolers would normally do). Because things simply *aren't* normal.

For the writers among you, the words will let you know when they're ready to be written. Write to your friends and family. Write your grocery list. Write what you're grateful for. Keep a journal. Or don't. This is new for all of us. Again, the words will come.

No matter where you fall in the homeschooling or writing spectrum, know that all feelings are okay. It's okay to grieve and mourn our losses. It's also okay to go bonkers and dance on the coffee table, or binge-watch *The Mandalorian* on Disney Plus. And, of course, stay safe. Wash your hands. Take care of each other.

Imagining a Cat on a Bed

CLARE CHODOS-IRVINE

· · · · · ● · · · ·

Our apartment is small, and everything lives inside handmade ceramics. I spend the mornings drinking cups of tea and cutting long, thin slices of sourdough. I eat them while watching a video about someone else who's stuck inside their own small apartment. It's quiet except for the wind, which is pushing through a small gap in my window. I can hear it whistling. I imagine a cat sitting on my bed, licking itself in the sunlight—except I didn't think ahead and get a cat before this started, so it's just a patch of sunlight and a pair of sweatpants I haven't put away yet.

The bathtub is broken again—or something. When I run the water in the bathroom sink, the drain in the tub goes *glug, glug, glug*, and I'm worried something terrible is going to spring out of it. I call my landlord. He tells me to plug all the holes except the tub drain and use a plunger to unclog it. I shove tampons and paper towels into the overflow holes, and plunge—and it works. It turns out my landlord is more helpful over the phone than when he shows up in person.

I spend much time walking around Westmount, because the most exciting thing I can do is walk around Westmount. I look at the houses, and take pictures of the ones that look haunted. I smell what people are cooking for dinner. I pick wildflowers out of people's front yards, knowing that someone is inside every house, watching me through the window as I look over my shoulder before clipping off a stem. I keep all of the tiny flowers in my palm. By the time I get back home, the fingers on my left hand are frozen.

I hang out with my roommate all evening. We watch *Lady Bird*, and it makes me miss my mom. My roommate thinks that's sweet, but then a moment later she must second-guess herself: She asks if my mom and I get along.

Every day feels like one of those Saturday afternoons as a kid, when we were having people over for dinner. It is always 3 pm. The house is spotless. I'm not allowed to watch TV, because my sister and I are supposed to watch a DVD later. I hang with my head over the side of my bed and let the blood rush to my face. I pretend to read a book. I go into the kitchen and bother someone who's cooking. I climb a tree, except it's not a tree—it's a fire escape. I hope my neighbour doesn't yell at me for being on the roof. The dinner guests never show.

Pandemic Blues

CAROLE THORPE

. . . .

South window with African Violet. Over Easter weekend, one solitary purple bloom. After Easter Monday, the bloom drooped, withered. I pinched it off, placed it in a blue-purple glass bowl that I made in Calgary, where I worked as a glassblower for many years.

The bowl sits on a small table shipped from Calgary. On the front right edge, a faded orange FRAGILE sticker reminds me that words melt, anneal, break open.

A month ago, as places closed down and events were cancelled, I began thinking about *The Journals of Susanna Moodie* by Margaret Atwood. I found excerpts in *Selected Poems: Margaret Atwood*. As a poet, I reread and internalize poems.

Standing near my FRAGILE Calgary Montreal table, I speak the lines from the introduction:

> *I take this picture of myself*
> *and with my sewing scissors*
> *cut out the face.*
> *Now it is more accurate:*
> *where my eyes were,*
> *every—*
> *thing appears*

I internalize and reflect on the power of these words a decade after returning east. I moved into my mother's condo in downtown Saint-Lambert in April 2010. I search for a photograph that captures that time in Saint-Lambert, when I struggled to work on my relationship with my mother. I took numerous photographs from her sixth-floor penthouse condo.

Sunshine lights up my second-storey condo in Côte-Saint-Luc: a cure for Pandemic Blues. I stand in my studio beside an oval table that once belonged to my mother. After she died in January 2013 in an NDG residence, this table became another studio table. Yesterday, I felt as if I were calling for her. Today, I feel I am calling for her. Yesterday, I placed a small clear paperweight with a carved hummingbird on the table. My mother gave me the paperweight. And like the hummingbird, she was tiny.

I pace slowly and conjure up these words from *The Journals of Susanna Moodie*, noticing the transformation that happens when shifting from reading to speaking:

Journal 1 1832-1840
FURTHER ARRIVALS
After we had crossed the long illness
that was the ocean, we sailed up-river
On the first island
the immigrants threw off their clothes
and danced like sandflies
We left behind one by one
the cities rotting with cholera,
one by one our civilized
distinctions
and entered a large darkness.

In this resurrected studio, crammed with books, art materials, sketchbooks, projects, unwrapped and repurposed, I roll out my yoga mat. Tadasana, Mountain pose. Decluttering the space seems impossible after several moves.

It's early afternoon. I finish a light lunch—an open-faced turkey sandwich, cheese, lettuce with carrots, potato chips. My audiologist calls from the Mackay Centre, across from Loyola Concordia. I've had severe hearing loss since I was two years old. He wants to know how my hearing aids are working. I explain that they are working well, and I bought extra hearing aid batteries.

I ask for guidelines for disinfecting my hearing aids. I'm not wearing them when I pick up the phone on my left side, because my right ear has lost the most.

This afternoon, I will befriend my hearing aids. I will insert them and recite *The Journals of Susanna Moodie*. Will this redirect the process of transformation, from reading to speaking to drama?

My afternoon recital begins:

> *THE PLANTERS*
> *They move between the jagged edge*
> *of the forest and the jagged river*
> *on a stumpy patch of cleared land...*

I look out my studio window. Apartment buildings, cars, roads disappear. Instead, fields, forests, planters, birds, animals. With my aids, I can hear everything in this new wilderness. Chirping birds overwhelm my ears with music.

The Pandemic and the Outsider

ANDI STEWART

· · · · · · · · ·

"**K**orean man stabbed near NDG," the headline on my cell phone read. "Attack believed to be racially motivated. Suspect under investigation." Similar stories had been appearing in the news with greater frequency. They contributed to the construction of a new reality that began just two weeks ago—a world in which terms like "viral load," "quarantine," and "social distancing" entered into common usage.

I finished the article and tossed my phone aside. I shook my head. Surely that can't happen here.

I took comfort in the idea of a multicultural Canada. This wasn't the United States. Surely we don't have their problems with race. I reflected on my own experience as a visible minority. I'd never had to suffer the trauma of aggressive and active bigotry, although there have been uncomfortable moments—situations in which I have been made to feel different. I've always attributed these instances to ignorance, the cycle of mimicked prejudice that runs through families and culture. Offensive jokes, yes. Head taxes, no. However, the line between passive and active racism is thin. Could this pandemic be pushing some to cross it? I shook my head again and rose from bed. I needed to buy groceries.

Looking out the window, I saw an overcast day. Spring and fall are unpredictable seasons in Montreal. I never know how to dress—in view of the temperature, will this outfit be too warm, or not enough? In view of the pandemic, will this outfit hold up to repeated washes? In view of safety, will this outfit invite conflict? I recalled videos of

186

Asian Canadians being confronted about their role in "bringing the 'China Flu.'"

I took a deep breath, settled on a bulky black sweater and jeans. "That couldn't happen to me," I thought.

Having finished getting ready, I checked the mirror. I saw myself and stood still for a few moments. Was I really ready? I uttered a quiet expletive in response. I took my glasses off, put in contact lenses, slid on sunglasses, despite the weather. I tied a scarf around my nose and mouth. I tucked my hair in a toque. My face at last covered, I found the tallest boots I possessed.

Closing front door, walking down the steps, I wondered if I'd covered up enough of my ethnicity to be safe. As an immigrant child and visible minority, I've learned that I am more easily accepted when I hide or abandon characteristics of my ethnic self.

In this new normal, the stakes feel higher. It isn't about acceptance anymore, but safety. There is more than one danger for me out there: the danger of catching the virus and the danger of standing out.

Listening to Your Gut

MARIE TULLY

· · · · · · · · ·

We are entering our fourth week of social distancing and confinement. My husband and I started social distancing two weeks before it was recommended. When I heard what was happening in Wuhan in December (2019), my gut started talking. My gut is rarely wrong. We cancelled appointments involving big crowds of people, concerts, and suppers with our gang of friends, because some of them were returning from vacations outside of the country. My gut told me to sit up and take stock of the situation. Everyone in my entourage thought we were a little paranoid, but I knew something was coming—something unbelievably big.

Here we are three months later, confined to our homes. Many, if not most, parts of the world are doing the same thing. It's oddly comforting to realize that you suddenly have much in common with everyone else in the world.

The restrictions have not changed our lives much. We take walks, meet neighbours we have never seen, even after thirty-eight years living in the same home. Our neighbours are nice. Obviously, we are all grappling with the situation related to the coronavirus, but some have grandkids the same ages as ours, some know people we know. Some have unique jobs, and some are loving retired life, as are we. So, walking, chatting with people (at a distance, of course), watching too much news, shopping online—it's all largely okay. We have an acre and a half of property, and so it's an absolute joy to be out there and work in the gardens. During inclement weather, we gladly stay inside. My husband retreats to his painting studio, and I work on my novel and other book projects (each grandchild gets his or her own picture book, written and illustrated by Grandma and Grandpa). We can quite easily wait it out, having a high old time every single day.

There's only one hitch. (Of course, there had to be a hitch.) The thing is, the coronavirus will kill me if I ever get it. Those chronic diseases—diabetes, heart disease, lung disease (as in COPD and asthma)—I have them all. Of course, I'm scared. If it weren't for that hitch, this whole thing would be a piece of cake. But dammit, I'm not ready to give it all up yet. I want more time—more time with my grandchildren, and my kids, more time with my husband, and our gang. I want more time for writing, more time in my brand new garden house/writing studio. I still have so much to say. So I'm going to wait it out, for as long as it takes.

Leaving France in the Time of COVID-19

RITA POMADE

· · · · · · · · ·

We were living in the centre of France in a small village outside Orléans when the news first broke about COVID-19 raging through Italy. I had a twinge of discomfort, but I believed it would be contained. When it hit a town on the French border, my partner and I still felt safe. The house belonged to his deceased mother. We were reluctant to see the writing on the wall, having just arrived for a six-week stay.

By the time we were confronted by the gravity of our situation, our airline had stopped running, and the nearest airport had closed. The only airport functioning was the Charles de Gaulle outside Paris—three hours away by car. By chance, we managed to secure one of the remaining flights on Air Transat, but we had no idea how we'd get to the airport. All buses, trains, and shuttles had stopped running. Drivers needed permits documenting one of two reasons for being on the road: for work, or as a divorced parent driving a child.

After numerous phone calls, we managed to find a driver with a permit who, for an obscene fee, was willing to show up at 5 am. I spent a sleepless night wondering if he'd find the house in this small village, or if he would he come at all, and if not, how would we get out?

On March 23, he arrived on time, at 5 am as promised, and drove like a madman to get us to the airport in half the time. He wiped down our luggage cart with disinfectant before driving off—an extremely gracious gesture that made up for the hair-raising ride.

We donned our masks and gloves before entering the cavernous Charles de Gaulle Airport, and found the place devoid of life. The only sound was our voices asking for directions to Terminal 1—

the only one open. Every so often a person drifted by in mask and gloves, looking equally lost. There were no personnel to be found until we reached our terminal. The scene was eerie and unsettling. I wondered if there really were a plane waiting for us.

We passed through customs alone. Soon other travelers started to appear in the waiting area—each masked and silent, keeping their six-foot distance until we boarded.

The Airbus, less than a third full, permitted us to spread out. We sat apart, wearing our masks, staring straight ahead, looking like extras in a dystopian film. Regular flight meals couldn't be served due to the epidemic. A steward laden with plastic bags, each containing frozen Mexican salads, Pringles potato chips, and small packets of truffles, tossed the bags onto our laps and disappeared. We passed the time waiting for our salads to thaw, and wondering what would await us in Montreal. But it didn't matter. We would be home.

The Birds Are Singing the Blues

ALEXANDRE MARCEAU

· · · · · **·** **·** **·** · ·

There's a stretch of water that separates the last sheets of ice between home and the island across the way. Birds line up where the ice begins, singing the blues. There are two decrepit houses on that island. Kayaking there in the summer reveals their sullied foundations from past floods. But the birds don't seem too concerned with any of it at the moment. They are closer than six feet apart, hopping over each other or gliding in the cold current.

I've been sitting here for hours, reading *Death in the Afternoon*.

The light coming in through the ceiling-high windows keeps shifting. The sun, like a slow merry-go-round, is completing its trajectory across the sky, as clouds slowly gather in the East.

I keep glancing over the page to look at the birds perched on the ice.

Are they mocking me?

I mark my page with a pen and toss the book on the table in exchange for my harmonica.

Can I have this dance?

But the birds are on the other side.

It is 7 pm.

I head out to skateboard around the neighbourhood, catching the last sweep of dusk, dodging impulsive gusts of wind. The streetlights, not yet accustomed to the early spring light, have been on for roughly an hour.

How odd, the machinations of the body. Without thinking, I arrive at a familiar house—her old house, the girl I dated nine years ago. I used to bring her dinner and we'd kiss. I didn't have to leave it on the porch and step back to the end of the driveway. She'd come out and whisper, "My dad is drunk." I knew that, in two hours, when he lay on the couch in the fetid living room, she would pick up his twelve empty Sleeman bottles and put them in the garage. He'd collect his consignment at the end of the week.

The clouds are like bulls in a parade—*running*. Her father's car is in the driveway, and I wonder if he is drinking himself out of shape tonight.

I light a cigarette, hear the faint doleful whispers of birds in the trees. Turning toward home, I notice lonely cars in driveways, wonder how the pandemic is affecting their owners. Are they like me, stuck on a couch reading? The current still moves. The economic God may be in peril, but I am lucky to have a house.

I can hear the birds singing the blues, loud and clear, as the rain begins to fall.

Night Clouds

LIS MCLOUGHLIN

. . . .

As I write, the moon shines brightly. For the last two days, the predawn sky has been clear, and the moon illuminates clouds that quickly pass. So odd to see these extraordinary night-time clouds acting exactly the same as mundane day-time ones. Somehow, I anticipate a certain degree of stealth, but no, they sail by quietly, dignified and white as their normal daytime selves. This strikes me as eerie—their boldness in lurking across the dark sky vulnerable to the stars, the universe, not waiting for Earth's atmosphere to turn opaque in the sun, to enclose them in a softly sheltering backdrop of blue or grey.

At this time, we can't see most people's faces, my friends half-hidden under their masks even outdoors as we walk. The boldness of these night-time clouds makes me feel small and happy, as if Nature were asserting her timelessness, taking over again from human tampering, as if there were a post- to this little apocalypse.

So far, we're surviving here okay, and I am as grateful as ever for the woods by which I am surrounded. My urban friends are not so lucky. They write to me of how the human-centred world has failed them. How the crowded streets are a menace. How they are stranded in domestic boxes in too close proximity. How they long for the open air.

And I picture them as clouds. And wish them freedom of the day and night, an acknowledgement or discovery of the essential in them that does not change. And I hope they can find what I am fortunate to have: earth and sky, with all the animate creatures therein—day and night.

Who Cares if I Smell?

EMILY BROWN

· · · · ● ● · · ·

The day starts as it always has since my thyroid was removed, with a small blue pill placed on my tongue and washed down with water. Only now, when I glance at the remaining pills, stacked at the bottom of their little pot, I remember I am reliant on a drug to keep me alive. What if society collapses, pharmacies turn to wastelands, and I'm forced to start breeding pigs for their thyroids? It seemed like a pretty implausible possibility four years ago.

My partner, just visible through the mess of duvet, blankets, and pillows, is, as usual, already scrolling through the news on his phone. The only difference—there's only one subject in the news.

I put on a T-shirt and shorts from two days ago. Who cares if I smell? I walk through to the lounge and pump up the back tire of my exercise bike, place my laptop on a nearby desk, plug in headphones, and pedal my way to Missouri, where Marty Byrde is having his toe nails ripped off. Just a usual day in *Ozark* of HBO.

At least watching TV apart gives my partner and me something to talk about, aside from the obvious. For the last few weeks, we've spent nearly every moment of the day together. Exceptions include the couple of trips I've had to make into the office, occasional walks around the block, and, of course, trips to the toilet. We work at separate desks in the same space, we eat together, we sleep together. I couldn't be more grateful.

Quitting time rolls around, and, since I'm off dinner duty tonight, I start on my daily physiotherapy exercises. Were I permitted to spend more time outside, my knee probably wouldn't allow it. Six months into recovery from a knee realignment surgery, there are days I wonder if life will ever be normal again.

Finally, having done my exercises and stretches, I join my partner on the sofa for more TV, a pack of frozen sweetcorn resting on my knee. Waiting for me by the bedside is a small, irritatingly pink pill. What other shade for a drug meant only for women? I had hoped to stop taking it soon. But if ever there were a right time for that big life decision, it isn't now.

Swinging Between Hope and Despair

LINDA THOMPSON

. . . .

Since quarantine began on March 16, I've noticed a pattern: One day I feel hopeful, and the next I crash. The weather can also change like that. So, when I open my eyes to the sound of pelting rain, I wait for crushing despair. Instead, acceptance settles in my bones. For today, at least, I am the lamb faithfully believing that the shepherds of our collective health will lead us to better days.

I use an unexpected burst of energy to keep busy, while my husband, Ben, an accountant, works from his home office. First, I make soup, grateful for a task that keeps my hands moving. I peel, chop, and cook carrots, celery, and onions. I add basil and oregano, then add chicken stock. The fragrance of the herbs and vegetables filling the house is comforting, as is knowing that the soup will nourish our bodies and our souls.

The phone rings. My son Erik, says: "I'm going to swing by after lunch to leave documents Ben needs for my taxes."

I feel a jolt of happiness. For a moment, I forget I won't be able to hug him, or ask him in, or even get closer than six feet. I never thought I'd see the day when I couldn't let one of my children into my home. With that realization, my heart shatters.

Both my children are single and living on their own. I worry about their physical and mental health during this interminable quarantine. They tell me they are fine. I believe them, but I long to see for myself.

Ben is Erik's stepfather. He is in the population considered vulnerable to COVID-19. He carries extra weight, is diabetic, and has high blood pressure. I tell him Erik is coming over, ask him if he's comfortable with that. "Or would you prefer I tell him not to come?" With the question, I break down. I see the same anguish on Ben's face.

"I can't do it," he says. "I can't tell him *not* to come."

The burden of responsibility for our health nonetheless triumphs, and I call Erik. I know my son is a rational adult, but logic has no place here. Emotions rule. I am so afraid he will be hurt that my voice trembles. "You know you won't be able to come in the house, right?"

"Mom, of course I'm not coming in!" he says. "I'm quarantining too, and if somehow I were responsible for making you or Ben sick, I couldn't live with myself." Relief floods through me and, just like that, I am happy again. I will see my son. We will be six feet away from each other on my front porch, but I will see him. I am grateful for that small privilege.

Masking the Truth

MIRIAM S. PAL

. . . .

My masquerade begins. I wipe off my red lipstick, unfold the mask over my nose and under my chin. I'm careful the elastics do not get ensnared in my earrings as I slide the straps over my ears. Wearing a mask in public is my new routine. Exiting the car, I notice many faces are covered.

Masks are part of the new pandemic parlance. The Rolls Royce of masks? The N95! Does anyone alive *not* know what "PPE" stands for? Sewing homemade fabric masks is the new hip lockdown hobby. It's cool to have a sewing machine. I heard there is a worldwide shortage of elastic. Mere months ago, it was a rare sight to see a mask-covered face on the streets of downtown Montreal. Today, they're everywhere, even at my suburban Canadian Tire parking lot.

A final check in the car mirror. My mask, which I sewed myself, has turquoise polka dots and navy blue bows. It goes with my outfit. A pandemic fashion statement. It's cold for mid-April, so I'm wearing a hat. The bottom half of my face is obscured by fabric. My eyes, framed by glasses, dominate my face.

The reflection in the mirror is a little unfamiliar. She looks like she is wearing a *niqab*, or even a *burqa*. Although I am a Muslim, half Pakistani, and have spent considerable time in Pakistan, I've never worn, or even tried on a veil. So this is how it feels: a little suffocating.

Waiting for my garden soil and mulch, my thoughts go back to last year. The news was all about Bill 21 (now a Quebec law), which bans religious face and head coverings among public-sector

199

employees. In 2020, secular face coverings are worn for health reasons, backed up by science.

Masks are increasingly a part of our daily pandemic lives. As of today, you cannot board an airplane without one. I wonder, what does the woman who wears a *niqab* do? Remove her religious face covering and replace it with a medically mandated face covering?

I smile at the harried Canadian Tire clerk bringing my purchases to the car. Why doesn't she smile back? But then I remember she can't see my mouth. I think of veiled women I've encountered in Pakistan. They are experts in nonverbal expression, using their eyes to convey messages. In the pandemic era, is this a new communication skill I should learn?

My car smells of cedar mulch. I slam the trunk closed and thank the clerk with a pandemic farewell—stay safe! Driving away, I turn on the radio in time to catch the Quebec premier's answer to a journalist's question: "Face masks are not part of Quebec culture..."

Author's note: *Starting July 18, 2020, Quebec required that all persons aged twelve and over wear a mask or face covering in enclosed or partially enclosed public spaces.*

Everything Is Normal and Nothing Is

SYLWIA BIELEC

· · · · · · · · ·

Day 14. You think it's about the isolation, but it's not. I already worked at home. With my daughter around, I am less alone than before. It's almost fun, like a weird, tense vacation. I don't have face-to-face meetings that need to be conveyed by email. As a Gen-X latchkey kid, I am well equipped to handle both aloneness and boredom, although I am rarely afflicted by the latter.

Addendum: Cooked two meals and made one snack. We took two walks, did a workout from YouTube. A full day of work, including a meeting in which people just needed to talk about their new lives. Sent a bunch of follow-up emails. Texted my mom. Bought a gift online. Everything is normal—and nothing is.

Day 15. Most days go by surprisingly fast. People don't seem to want to end online meetings, as if our little Zoom-tiled wall of faces were holding us up. Had to mute the local parents' group—parents calling out other parents for taking their little ones to deserted parks for a few minutes, possibly taking precautions or not. *Did you see them near the slide?* Are they looking for someone to blame, when it comes? *It was so-and-so; I saw her and her kids at Dollarama, and they were touching the toys. It was them.* Or: *It was whosit, when he touched the carousel with his contaminated hands; he wasn't compliant. I saw him!*

Addendum: worked a full day, made two meals, pork roast, bought a baguette. Had ice cream. Took two walks.

Day 16. Spirits continue to roller coaster, as the first hopeful milestone is passed, and we contemplate the month ahead. We have lists. We have bursts of energy and ideas followed by a slow but sure sinking into lethargy. There is guilt at our moments of sloth, and there is relief that there are no witnesses. Everything matters and nothing does. We clutch our productive moments like lifebuoys. The sun on our faces is a benediction.

Addendum: Worked a full day, figured out some grade five math, hydrated, ate homemade roasted maple almonds. Cleaned the kitchen and bathroom. On our walk around the neighbourhood, my daughter called COVID-19 the "fucking stupid dick Coronavirus." I wonder where she learned all those swears.

The Joys of Lockdown: Coming Clean

ELISA ROBIN WELLS

· · · · · ● ● ● ● · ·

A confession: it might sound weird or even callous but, in some ways, I'm enjoying the shutdown. The noise outside my apartment has lessened. I like the lack of expectation to go out or do anything.

Once I stopped working, grocery shopping and walking became my only excursions. Walking around my Côte-des-Neiges neighbourhood, I saw squashed plastic water bottles on the edges of roads, tucked under hedges, and littering every public grassy area.

I noticed seemingly endless empty Tim Hortons and McDonald's cups, and an assortment of plastic bottles and gloves. I wasn't the only one. A friend's Facebook post mentioned plastic gloves strewn about everywhere. It was even on the news.

So I started picking up empty water bottles. Within a couple days, I'd ordered a picker tool. The following week I was prepared. I tied my hair into a ponytail, put on plastic gloves and with my grabber tool in one hand and the reusable bags in the other, I marched outside.

But what if somebody noticed me picking up trash on the side of the road? Wouldn't they think I was a weirdo? Luckily, not many people were outside, and those who were either didn't look my way, or they walked on the other side of the street. Again, this shutdown was working for me. I could clean up without people gawking.

As I picked up discarded gloves, I imagined I was stopping a child from touching them. As I grabbed bottles, crushed cans, plastic wrappers, and containers, I hoped I was helping someone who couldn't leave their house. I dreamed of picking up every plastic water bottle and recycling them all.

Yet people did notice. One woman asked me where I purchased my grabber and commended me for what I was undertaking. When I walked toward a littered area behind a hospital, a woman leaned out her window. She had seen me before and wanted to tell me what a great job I was doing. When I headed home with bags full of recyclable glass and plastic, a man on a scooter smiled approvingly.

As I turned onto my street, the pile of garbage that had accumulated under a heap of cut branches was no longer there. The silver glitter of empty wrappers and stark blue bottle tops no longer affronted my eyes. When I walked along the wooded path behind the hospital, most of the litter was gone—because I had removed it.

Although I know I'm not solving our garbage or recycling problems, I'm doing something positive for others and for myself. After all, I don't want to see dirty coffee cups, water bottles, soda cans, disposable gloves, and masks on my walk in my neighbourhood or on a tree-lined street, and I'm sure other people don't want to see them either.

Going Shopping, or: War Preparations

ANABELLE ZALUSKI

. . . . ● ● . . ●

I pull my boots on, flatten my coat against my chest, and strap a mask across my face. Grocery shopping is an ordeal now, so I've learned to map such expeditions with the care and planning of a war. Do I have my list? The cart to pull behind me? Will I remember to keep my distance, and only pick up the apples that I plan on buying, instead of examining every one?

The kids downstairs have coloured uplifting messages and pasted them on the apartment door. They make me smile, even though they're not for me. I turn and drag my cart down our little concrete stairs.

I like my neighbourhood. One of my favourite houses has a wall of browned vines. I pray to no god in particular that they grow when spring arrives in May, with the certainty that April lacks. But the crocuses are growing at the feet of the trees, right where the roots melt into the soil.

The sun shines and the fresh air is nice. I walk on the bright side of the street. I wish I could smile through my mask, but instead I awkwardly lock eyes with people. I probably seem hostile. I could easily be grimacing, or sticking out my tongue. Is she okay? Maybe she stubbed her toe, or she is remembering something embarrassing. At a stoplight, I have to remember to breathe because, somehow, being still has become more stressful than moving.

I finally get to the Metro, and it's unusually dark inside. There's no line along the sidewalk. I feel cheated: Nobody told me it's closed on Sundays, as is the *Fruiterie* beside it, and the SAQ. I promised my roommate I'd buy more wine.

To make myself feel better, I decide to browse Jean Coutu for a few minutes, spend some money there. That's what I set out to do. I pick up a bottle of honey because we're out of it, some of those curly hair elastics, and a bag of Doritos. I also buy red lipstick, because it's on sale, and I've been thinking about it lately. Who needs lipstick during a global pandemic?

Walking home on Sherbrooke Street, I see women walk in big coats and sunglasses. They look like my mother. They have the same hair, shiny, dyed. My mom used to be a brunette, like me, but her hair is getting lighter. Every time I go home, it looks different.

I drag my embarrassingly empty cart behind me and turn the corner onto my street, cutting through the gas station. On our front door, the rainbows are still there. A page that says: "THANK YOU, DELIVERY WORKERS" has a corner peeling off. I press it down. It springs back up.

PENNING THE PANDEMIC
The Art of Connecting

JOEL YANOFSKY

. . . .

This self-isolation business is playing right into my hands. From the time I started thinking of myself as a writer, some forty years ago, I knew my main talent for the job lay in my ability to cut myself off from other people. In fact, it seemed to be the whole point of the endeavour.

So, yes, the solitude of the writing life has come naturally to me. In university, I never showed up in the library to work with classmates on my latest assignment; instead, I rushed home to do it. I don't get it when colleagues insist they're at their most creative in cafés. They're not writing, I mutter to myself; they're schmoozing.

I'm a second-generation loner and freelancer. My father, a sign-painter, worked in the basement of our suburban bungalow. I write in the basement of my home in NDG. A running joke dates back to my first days typing away at stories I was convinced no one would ever want, let alone pay for: you can't beat the commute, I assured my worried family and friends.

Or the dress code, which is to say there isn't one. I confess I used to be embarrassed answering the door in my work clothes (a.k.a. pyjamas) whenever a delivery person, say, showed up in the middle of a weekday afternoon. I never signed for anything without lying about how I was taking a sick day. But there's nothing to be embarrassed about any more. No need to lie either. Now, everyone just leaves the package on the porch and disappears. It's perfect. There's no one around to judge.

Of course, it can get lonely facing the blank page every day. That explains why I've jumped at every chance to speak at a school or a book club, or take on the closest thing I've ever had to a real job—teaching. My steadiest gig thus far has been leading a workshop for the Quebec Writers' Federation. The workshop, which focuses on the art of the memoir, has much to recommend it—from encouraging new writers, to hearing myself talk about my favourite subject (me). Most of all, it gets me out of the basement each spring for eight consecutive weeks.

This spring, due to a devastating virus, the job has come to my basement via Zoom—and so far, so good. Still, when I was first presented with the chance and the choice to meet with my students online, I admit I was sceptical.

Teaching memoir not only tends to, but is also intended to inspire writers to share their most personal stories. This means getting to know the people around you fast and learning to trust them even faster. And, while I've seen this kind of thing happen regularly at QWF workshops, it has happened at close quarters, twelve of us, just about shoulder to shoulder, around a circular table. I couldn't imagine a virtual workshop would be as well-suited to such an intimate undertaking.

Rick Moody, a novelist and creative writing professor at Brown University, also acknowledged his doubts in a recent *New Yorker* essay about teaching in the time of the pandemic. "The literary arts are more about a human in the room feeling something," he writes, "expressing it, and the other humans listening and ideally feeling similarly."

But, as it turns out, that ideal of "feeling similarly" comes naturally to humans, even when they're popping up on a computer screen, self-isolated in a variety of locations across the city. I should have known that what has happened so often before when my fellow writers and I were in the same room together would happen now that we're all on Zoom. We've reached consensus about the things that matter most—what makes a story work, what makes it touch us and teach us about ourselves and one another.

A writer's main job, I tell my Zoom-mates, is to pay attention. This workshop has made me pay attention to how human it is to crave consensus—and not just here in my virtual classroom, but everywhere. We're routinely and graciously doing things that would have seemed silly or aggravating just a couple of months ago—staying six feet apart, wearing masks and gloves, scrubbing down our groceries.

In another *New Yorker* essay about the pandemic, novelist Karen Russell writes, "This physical separation belies what is happening on another plane; people are responding to the crisis with a surprising unity."

But is it a surprise? Even for a writer like me, who started out wanting nothing more than to keep his distance, I always suspected that wasn't really my plan. The plan was to connect and, this strange spring, for two hours every week, thanks to QWF and my talented, patient Zoom-mates, that's what I'm doing. What we're all doing, together.

Under Control?

KAREN ZEY

• • • • • • • •

Today is Day 46. Two weeks since the clinic visit, and hubby is symptom free. The knot in my stomach eases. I scratch a check-mark on the kitchen calendar, then settle at the computer to write about my stress.

Day 1

I've got this. Hubby is a senior with chronic health conditions, and I'm a middle-of-the-night worrier. All we need is a plan, just like everyone else. Focus. I've got this. Two of us in self-isolation: check. Order groceries online: check. Lentils, root vegetables, tinned fruit, just in case: check. Brisk walks at a safe social distance: check. I am a loving, well-organized, do-everything-possible-to-keep-him-healthy kind of wife and—I've got this.

Days 2-25

Everything will be okay. Hubby and I settle into pandemic routine. Read, write, phone family and friends. Cook, tidy, Zoom with family and friends. Teach my library workshop online. Indulge (together) in too much Netflix. Obsessively watch the news (together), then limit the gloom broadcasts to once a day. Walk the neighbourhood (together) and look for rainbows in the windows. Read those pale-pink, mint-green, and sky-blue messages of hope that children have chalked on their driveways. Everything will be okay.

Day 26

The dermatologist calls. Hubby's January biopsy shows a small melanoma on his chest. Nothing serious. She'll remove it in the office. A routine, twenty-minute procedure. Postponing more than a couple of weeks is not a good idea. Okay, we'll come next Thursday at 8 am. First patient of the day. He can enter through the back door of the clinic. The doctor reassures us she'll be wearing a mask and gloves.

Worry slams into my gut. Not about the quarter-sized spot of cancer. He can survive that. But how many patients has the doctor seen in the last few weeks?

Day 32

We arrive early. The only car in the parking lot. I can't go in with him. I try not to sound like a nag, as I nag him about the protective steps he needs to take. Remember, hands off your mask. Purell if you touch anything. Call me and put me on speaker phone, so I can listen to the steps for post-procedure care.

Hubby is patient as I go over this. He knows it will calm me down. Twenty minutes later, he's out. She's frozen him twice. Didn't hurt too much. He takes off his paper mask in the car and puts it in the plastic bag I've brought along. He Purells thoroughly. When we get home, he changes clothes and washes his hands. Any viruses on his skin vanquished by that twenty-second swirl of soap and hot water.

But any airborne viruses in the doctor's breath—they could already be travelling inside his body, invisible for up to fourteen days.

I begin the countdown until Day 46, until I can say it again: I've got this.

Sending Down Messages of Hope

ALISON PIPER

. . . .

The pink supermoon rises quickly in a golden blaze, as if in a hurry. Its white facial features come into full view as night falls. This heavenly beacon shines down on the rainbow-lit structures of pandemic Montreal. The new Champlain Bridge, the Olympic Stadium, the downtown office towers, and the Montreal Biosphere are glowing with red, orange, yellow, green, blue, indigo, and violet light—a message of hope to the city, to me.

Or so I imagine. I watch the moon from my six-foot-wide second-storey windows. Like everyone else, I am not allowed to leave my NDG neighbourhood. Like everyone else, I am also a little afraid to leave my apartment, or to go too far.

Some friendly lights flick on in bedrooms of the mansion across the street. Perhaps the inhabitants also want to have a look. Or maybe they are weary and getting ready for bed.

I pull my coat on, go down the stairs and out the door to take photos. My cold fingers fumble with my cell-phone camera, flexing the screen wider to take a closer shot. I take several photos and check them. The moon's beauty and grandeur prove to be elusive. Dissatisfied, I give up. I'll simply try to remember how the supermoon looked. Someone else will post an impressive photo on the internet, and I'll settle for that.

Soon, Jupiter appears in the night sky, becoming the second brightest object. More planets and stars join the display. They look like they are pulsing on and off. Are they really, or is it an optical illusion?

There is no one on the street, but the lone bagpiper has come out again. Tonight, he's playing "Amazing Grace." It's haunting, yet comforting somehow. I feel less alone and try to follow the sound of the bagpipes, hoping to find him. I think I am getting closer, but suddenly the sound stops. Perhaps he has gone inside; perhaps he became cold.

I walk back to my apartment. There is still no one around. Climbing the stairs, I'm thankful for the warmth emanating from the vintage steam radiators. At least the friendly lights across the street are still on. The supermoon and Jupiter are keeping me company.

On Waking

LOUISE HINTON

· · · · · · · ·

On waking:
   What day is it?
Enough sleep, car gone
Rainbows, a cup of tea, the ticking clock
Blueberry pancakes, pretending it's the weekend
Working from home while daughter's still asleep
Office banter on Teams, cold sunshine across the desk
Mommy, where's the glue gun?
Ping! A Messenger message from my brother in isolation
Ping! A Teams message from the coordinator:
Can you translate this by 3 pm?
Me: LOL
Ping! No, *srsly*, 3 pm at the absolute latest
Mommy, I can't find the X-Acto knife
No knives!
Hey Mom, can you hold this while I paint the back? No! Don't put
it down until it dries.
That's enough screen time. Why are you watching YouTube? Why?
Well, I was making magic potion, but I spilled the dye
Is it still Monday?
Mommy, I'm bored.
Clean the litter box and sweep the floor
Bored people will be assigned a chore
Wipe up that paint. Is that glue on the door?
Go outside.
Breathe.

Is that a snowflake?
Fluttering laundry on the optimistic clothesline casts shadows on the sleeping garden.
Ping! This job is more urgent! I need it by 4!
Ping! Ping! Ping!
Silence notifications.
Vibrate. Did you get my text? Cancel that first translation. We don't need it anymore.
She imitates her teacher dancing
We giggle madly
Mommy, this was the best moment of the coronavirus vacation.
Evening:
Sweetheart home safe from essential services work
Writing in my rocking chair
Tea in a fine clay pot
A secret: I love being home with my family.
A sigh released from the channel of sighs, where all the weariness goes.

Answer Me This

ANNE LEWIS

· · · · · • · · · ·

Well, and so, I have said it all—is it not enough? All the sharp words blunted—were they not enough? The idle engine chuckling—was it not sufficient? The frozen badlands kicking me in the tucked chin—were they not allowed to shut me up? Nope.

"Go get your head examined," she said. In the flowering embers, fireside chatty she was. Head inclined, hair all furry, hat askew, she was. Piece of amber, she was.

"I'll ask you the same," I said. Why should I fill up her space for her? Answer me that. Before all this, I was never this way. It pressured up. Funny enough, that's what I expected. The comeuppance of it all. Those were the days of honey, and aspirin, and any kind of beetle juice. Are they all gone now? Answer me this. Is it to lament at our watching and cowering? Is it to be still at our alone-ing and shushing? Is it to be spiking fevers at our vigilance and philosophizing? Answer me. Used to be I could write with a whole clatter around me, but now, tear open a flimsy bag in the same room, and I will shoot you a look.

"I'm trying to make sense," I will say. On the flat wasteland, the car has broken down. Sitting on a prickly, red tartan blanket, my dad will look at me like I'm daft. My mum will raise her thermos cup lid to me by its little handle. "Good luck to you," she'll say. Slices of turf are stacked by the road, molten wet like phosphorus, a metal so soft you can slice it with a dinner knife. The careful wind tickling at my nose will be pointing to where the sense is. Wasn't I wild with excitement that day at the school chemistry bench to discover those little grey slabs on a dish were not a butter of sorts?—they were phosphorus, a metal at room temperature.

If I were at a different temperature, what would I be? Pigeon wing? Salty wave? Lion's claw? Rumpelstiltskin awakening to a...

A Suitcase Full of Black Clothes

DORU LUPEANU

· · · · · · · · ·

My father died.

I wish I were capable of using metaphors and making this statement more gut-wrenching, closer to what I feel than the three-word phrase that seems to beg for attention and compassion. Yet, I can't express myself beyond these three words.

It's been more than a month. Forty-six days to be more precise, right at the height of the lockdown. He died from heart failure, in a different country but close to the rest of my family.

I turned robot-like at the news. I bought a suitcase, a plane ticket, and two black shirts, and I started packing. The earliest flight would have been the day after his death. And then it hit me: I would be stuck in an imposed quarantine for two weeks, unable to see anybody. My robot self collapsed to make room for a sobbing child who was initially denied the right to grieve.

Time heals, they say. And I guess, in some respect, it makes any problem live in the past to which it belongs. As the sobbing subsided, I tried to remember him for his life and not his last moments. I focused on household chores and little distractions to keep my mind busy.

Until today.

I decided to clean my closet. Tucked inside was a suitcase full of black clothes; the reminder unleashed mute pain. I've been staring at it ever since, trying to find comfort in the idea that time will push suffering into the past. But all I can think of is...

My father died.

Lining Up Those Ducks

FRANCESca M. Lodico

. . . .

"I got my ducks," says Lissa on the phone. "I'm their momma."
Lissa used to live next door with her wire-haired dachshund,
Ginger. For five years, we shared the neighbourly camaraderie of single
creatives bound by solitude: our "before" version of together alone.

All perky ears and springy neck, Ginger was scrappy. She barked
above her weight and was a conduit for Lissa's own misadventures. The
yip&yap of Lissa&Ginger were part of the soundtrack of my building,
their escapades part of the lore of our little corner of Outremont.

Although Lissa&Ginger moved out last year, I have missed them
most acutely during confinement. When Lissa emailed me last week
about *Photocopie Zoubris*, a Mile End/Outremont hub on Parc Avenue, it made me yearn for Demetra and Jimmy (Zoubris), and for the
community outside my window:

> zoubris still closed mamma mia…
> honey
> do you think you could print these two pages
> eeee!
> love and hugs!

I am a writer, and I live alone. Isolation comes easy to me. But
right now, the story of my day often hinges on these moments of
connectivity over the phone. The musicality in Lissa's voice is punctuated by woofs and *sotto voce* quips. "My ducks! One—I call her

219

'Isabella'—is perfectly insouciant. The other one, Vinnie Russo, is all 'Hi, I'm gorgeous!'" she says.

Lissa still lives in the neighbourhood. She tells me she's been bringing the ducks at Parc Beaubien alfalfa and oats, "healthier than crumbs of bread or popcorn." They forage well, but Isabella's making her eggs now, so this gives her an extra kick.

"Isabella will gently paddle to one of the tufts and be like, 'What you got?' I toss her a few sprigs and she swallows them. Vinnie lets her eat first. He's always checking on his girl. He'll come over to me for a quick 'quack' and dart straight back to her. Nature-triggered hormones: testosterone, estrogen, love."

Lissa feels a responsibility to be optimistic, because "so many people are suffering." The parks are empty but "today a boy, no swings or sandbox, no kids to play with, noticed the ducks. *Tu as vu le canard, maman, le canard!*' He was learning about nature, about himself."

The ducks "have no clue" about the pandemic, says Lissa, but they know a thing or two about survival. When it gets hot in summer, the pond in Parc Beaubien can dry up so "the mother will take her chicks to Parc Outremont or Parc Saint-Viateur in the middle of the night when there are no people or cars." Lissa chuckles. "Waddling up Bloomfield Avenue, all in a straight line."

After fifteen and a half years together, Lissa lost Ginger to natural causes in December. "I dreamed that she said to me: 'Be happy.' Ginger's soul exists. Her light is beaming out onto the world."

Before we get off the phone, Lissa offers advice: "My friend, get yourself some oregano oil at [Santé] Thuy. Immune support for the respiratory system. Good for the body."

Lissa&Ginger&Isabella&VinnieRusso: good for the soul.

The New Normal

REBECCA MORRIS

. . . .

It's been six weeks since the schools shut down, six weeks since my husband started working from home. I used to write during the day, when the house was empty and quiet. Now the house is never empty. It's only quiet in the early mornings, while my teenage children are still asleep.

For the first few weeks of quarantine, I flailed. I floundered. I couldn't read, couldn't write, couldn't think. At last, I've settled into this strange new normal, carved out a new writing routine.

I'm at my desk by 7:30 am. Three longhand morning pages to empty out my brain, ten minutes of Headspace meditation to soothe my stressed-out soul, then I'm writing. Well, revising: this novel I've been working on for years is nearly done.

Today, I'm working on chapter nine. One of my main characters is visiting her grandmother in a nursing home. The book is set in 2004, so I push away the dreadful thoughts of present-day nursing homes, overwhelmed with COVID-19 infections. This scene is already written, but it needs to be tightened, sharpened.

I get to work. I cut sentences, stitch together paragraphs, add details. The nursing home attendant has a name now: Habiba. The scene comes into focus. I dig into my character's motivations, emotions, memories. I am lost in the world of my novel.

I glance at the clock: 9:30 am. I need to wrap this up, wake my children. I polish a few more sentences, save the file. I hoped to finish this scene, to move onto the next chapter tomorrow. I'm not there yet. Disappointed, I shake my head, stand up, stretch my stiff back.

My black lab is waiting patiently outside the door. I pet the dog, wake the kids. For the rest of the day, domestic life will dominate. Online math with my thirteen-year-old twins. Laundry. Mailing cards to my mother in Ontario, my aunt in London, England. When will I see them again? I FaceTime a local writer friend, and we commiserate about the difficulties of novel writing. My sixteen-year-old daughter wants to talk about writing, too; she's working on a long fanfiction piece, over 35,000 words already. She has been writing only since the quarantine began. I am amazed by her enthusiasm and her creativity. I go for a run—it feels wonderful to exercise in the sunshine. I am so lucky to be healthy, to have my healthy family. I worry about my parents, about my in-laws, about all the beloved older people in my life. I need a dinner plan. Not pasta; we've eaten that two days in a row. Homemade pizza? Perfect. Tonight, I might start a new puzzle, or we may watch something on Netflix. I'll read more *Anne of Green Gables* to my sons, go to bed by ten. I'm already looking forward to tomorrow, to another writing day.

Do I Sing or Nap?

JILL LESLIE SAPPHIRE-GOLDBERG

· · · · · ● · ● · · · ·

I hear the songbird in the predawn. As usual, I slept with the window open. I believe the cold helps me sleep more deeply, and I really need it. I doze, because I can. There's a thick, carless silence, even though I live in town. I've become used to it. When I finally awaken, the sun is streaming into my room. I actually get out of bed. However, I'm aware of the word for what I'm feeling: depression. I'm even getting accustomed to cycles through the week.

I was working up north in Quebec's subarctic with the Naskapi on March 13, when everything came to a screeching halt. The school there was suddenly closed, and I was sent home to Quebec City and into quarantine. I've not been in public since then, except for occasional walks. I live alone. I have a son in Quebec City whom I cannot see and a daughter who fled China where she was working and has hunkered down in Laos with her Nigerian boyfriend, a medical student.

In fairness, I'm usually fine with my solitude; after all, to a certain extent, I have chosen to live this way. However, these days, since moving beyond those first weeks of feeling alternately scared and immobilized by not recognizing the world, my solitude feels heavy with loneliness. Perhaps it is odd: I'm quite functional during the week. My work on behalf of the Naskapi is intense, fascinating, and demanding, and it provides structure to my days; it keeps me going. When the week ends, the thundering silence produces moments of enchantment—hearing something as "normal" as songbirds or the geese flying overhead, the sight of the Full Pink Moon, or some dusty ground where grungy snow recedes. I'm engaging in self-care;

I meditate and make healthy food choices. Still, I cannot shake the sadness and depression that stay with me all day.

I think of my eighty-three-year-old father in Florida—his advanced Parkinson's leaving him frail, the doctor says. I weep. Will I see him again? I miss his wicked humour acutely. My eighty-one-year-old mother is in Vermont's Northeast Kingdom, but I cannot get to her either. I cannot even see my own son, as he is in a sort of constant quarantine as a result of the fragile health of his girlfriend's mother.

How did we get here, I wonder again, and how *will* we move forward? I make a pot of genmaicha using the tea set my son gave me when he was just a boy. I'm nostalgic for those easier days and realize how unexceptional I am in the end, how it really is "just" our common humanity uniting us. Grateful for what I had and have, I wish to retreat into sleep. Do I nap or sing?

#covidream

SHELLEY TEPPERMAN

. . . .

My apartment is in utter disarray, tornado-blown: clothes, mingled dirty and clean, everywhere. It's time to head to my (imaginary) office job. I need to pee, get dressed, but I can't find a bra can't find my underwear can't find shoes. *Didn't I fold a stack of underwear yesterday?*

My father's voice reverberates: "It's a pigsty in here."

I dig out a pair of knee-high boots, then realize they'll be too warm. *How long has the snow been gone?* There's a bolt of bright pink in one pile of clothes, a dress last worn in my twenties. Not quite clean, but it will do. I decide to forego panties (the dress is calf-length, no one will know) and eventually locate some low-heeled pumps. I still need a bra. There's only the ludicrously padded one that supported my sales-rack prom dress (the décolletage completely unsuited to my broomstick figure, but the price tag was acceptable to my father).

I smear and blend foundation on my face. I look like an unfinished android. Can't find my lipstick eyeliner telephone. I still need to pee but keep delaying, and it isn't helping. My husband decides to wait for me in the car.

I try to file my quarterly GST. My father, an accountant, taught me to do multiplication in my head but not how to do my taxes. Before pressing "send," I want to double check my figures, so I take screenshots in case the file doesn't save. Of course, it doesn't save. The numbers on the screenshots aren't visible. *Where are the numbers?*

It's time to leave for work. My husband's waiting, and I still haven't peed.

225

I give up on the GST, give up on eyeliner, decide to pee and search for lipstick in the bathroom.

I haven't fixed my hair, which is too long, so I clip it into a knot. Later, at work, I'll sneak into the bathroom and finesse it. I find the lipstick beside a chic grownup purse that always gives me shoulder pain. I hesitate between a backpack and the more professional hand-bag that seems too large and cumbersome for the few essentials I need.

In this dream, my husband resembles my father—gone for thirty-nine years. He has the patience of a saint, unlike my father, whom I've just started to write about. He is kind, generous, indulgent. I don't want to make my husband late for work. In real life, he doesn't work outside the house except when he travels.... I'm going to make him late. No doubt he understands, although he doesn't really. He just grasps that I am struggling, doesn't understand the disorder but accepts it, recalibrates for his impending lateness—he who hates to be late and always arranges his life to be early, he whose patience, kindness, and generosity have healed the father wound.

I awake dry-mouthed... get up to pee, drink water, write this dream down.

The Hard Part Is Yet to Come

DANIELLE WONG

· · · · · · · ·

My daughter asks me to stay beside her. At first, the reason is homework. When she's done, I get up to leave. She is not willing to let me go. She needs company to colour. I stay and colour with her, while we listen to music. Some weeks, it is "Lean on Me"; other times, it is "You Lift Me Up" or "Amazing Grace." She plays the song of the week over and over, repetition the one thing she understands completely.

Sudden outbursts of anger toward everyone or streams of tears erupt around the same time of the day. This is the time of day that used to be reserved for letting go of everything she was holding in from school, all her frustrations at herself for having so much trouble understanding the material or what her peers are saying, all her exhaustion from socializing, from taking public transportation in the morning and the afternoon. This time is for all her frustration at losing independence, not seeing her friends and teachers in person. She does see them on various platforms. She listens more than she speaks, but, when she speaks, her voice lights up and that time of day becomes a memory.

Movement and fresh air are important. She probably wouldn't move much if it weren't for her dance teacher posting moves for a dance, or the YMCA having an online exercise class through live chats.

I ask her to come out for a walk with me. She pulls out her phone and pulls up Google: "First instruction from Google: Stay Home." I ask if she wants to go biking. She turns her phone toward me: "First instruction from Google: Stay Home." How about badminton in the backyard? "Google says 'no!'" I explain to her that Google also has

227

a rule to get some fresh air. She is not sure if she should believe me, until her siblings tell her the same thing.

She tells me that she likes being home. She can see her friends on her phone. Homework is considerably less stressful when the teacher is not in the room. And there is much more time for dancing, drawing, colouring.

Finally, it hits me: The sudden transition from going to school every day to staying home every day is not the hardest part of this quarantine. Staying home, learning at home, going online to see teachers and friends—these are not the hardest parts either. The hardest part has yet to come. That part will involve trying to get my daughter back out the door to take public transportation to and from school, to be physically with all her classmates, and to be in the classroom to do her work with the teacher in the room.

Today's Tea Remedy for the Coronavirus

CAROLYNE VAN DER MEER

· · · · · · · · ·

I'm standing at the window. I'm on the eleventh floor of a high-rise. The world seems small from here. And when I look out, there's almost nothing going on. A few cars on the road, crawling along. It's like a Sunday in the 1970s. Except it's not—because this is every day. Since the virus arrived, it's like the world has been anaesthetized, and I can't help but wonder when—and how—it will wake up.

I look in the pantry. There's far too much tea in there. And it's not because I'm a hoarder. I didn't go out and buy truckloads of toilet paper. What was *with* that, anyway? I shake my head. What, you run out of food—and then, miraculously, increase your trips to the loo? People are strange.

My big problem is baking powder. Screw the toilet paper—we have plenty of that—but I can't get any bloody baking powder. I pull the Ahmad Aromatic Earl Grey tin out of the cupboard as I consider it all. So, people are making loaves of bread and bathroom trips. It makes no sense.

I use a spoon to pry off the lid of the tin and take a whiff. The bergamot overtakes my senses. Tea is my way out of this. I make cup after cup, day after day—all the while considering the baking-powder shortage. Seriously, there are about fifteen different types of Earl Grey in here—from Ahmad, to Fortnum & Mason, to Taylors of Harrogate, all promising something different. Then there are my sister-in-law's favourites—*Thé des Tsars* and Rooibos Samurai— brought as a thank-you gift back in the days when you could host a dinner party. I finger the smooth black tins, think back to those evenings of food and wine, laughter and conversation, and wonder if all that is a bygone era. Sometimes I feel like I'm walking through a post-apocalyptic novel, like there's no way out of the pages.

I put the lid back on the Ahmad tea and turn to the rooibos—open it, inhale the fragrance. It's a deep red mix with bits of dried orange zest. I imagine the Valencia orange groves I once visited in Spain. The bitter orange marmalade I smeared on toast in London cafés. Yes, tea is my way out of here. Out of the pages. I'll find my way home, eventually.

The Perils and Parallels of Listening to Bruce Springsteen's "Human Touch" in the Time of Pandemic

MARIAN REBEIRO

. . . .

It might sound a bit crazy, but I love a commute—a passive commute, mind you, where I can sit down on the bus or metro, and check out for a half hour, listen to music, read a book, or people-watch. I love people-watching. My morning commute gives me a moment to shift gears and to get in the zone (whatever "zone" I need to be in that day), after rushing to get myself ready and out of the house. It's a moment of stillness, even though I'm still technically moving as I get from point A to point B, and I love it. It's mine.

Not so during a pandemic lockdown.

These days, offices and public buildings are closed, and public transportation is (in my mind) out of bounds to everyone, except essential and front-line workers. I'm extremely grateful that I'm among those whose job situation merely shifted to working from home. It might've taken a couple weeks of adjusting and some furniture rearranging in the middle of the night, but it's certainly better than the alternatives that many others are facing. But no more commute means no more morning stillness. Suddenly, I don't know how to transition from "at home" mode to "at work" mode.

Add that to the growing list of global concerns, and all my Big Plans for the spring and summer being foiled across the board, and my brain overindulges in work to fill the sudden void where friends and family normally fit in.

In a pandemic lockdown, my brain is in constant work mode.

As remedy, in my isolation, I've manufactured a substitute commute by waking up and immediately putting on music. I usually listen to an entire album, or a short Spotify playlist, from start to finish. I know I could read a book or an article, or listen to a short podcast, but, as I work for a writers' federation, I feel that's too close to my job. So music is my way of getting into the zone.

This morning, I woke up with Bruce Springsteen's "Human Touch" in my head. I don't know why; I haven't listened to Bruce in a while, but I think: *Why not give in to my subconscious and put that record on?* The plight of the everyman works in a pandemic, too, right?

I think it worked a little *too* well, in this new, quarantined world, in which human touch has become the ultimate taboo:

> *You might need somethin' to hold on to*
> *When all the answers, they don't amount to much*
> *Somebody that you could just to talk to*
> *And a little of that human touch*

What was my subconscious thinking?

Suddenly, my new form of commuting reminds me of the very thing I've been trying to forget.

FINALE
Making It Meta

· · · · · · · · ·

RACHEL MCCRUM

'm woken at 5:30 am by our *petit pirate* of a cat batting a grey paw in my face. This is habitual. She doesn't want to be fed or to go out. Just give her a sign of life. She knows better than to touch J, my partner, sleeping peacefully beside me. His ability to flick a hip—and send her flying off the bed—without waking up should be patented.

I'm usually awake early these days. I like this pale time. I reach for my phone, check on the chat from family in hours-ahead Northern Ireland and England, from friends in Scotland. I skim the headlines of *The Guardian*. Today's big debate concerns Dominic Cumming's little jaunt to Durham during the UK lockdown, and whether Boris Johnson will have the guts to fire him (bet you a Montreal May heat-wave that he won't). Then I get to the *Montreal Gazette* and CBC. I always start with the news from home first. A hard habit to shake.

Today, I'm due to write the final episode for "Chronicling the Days." I've spent the past seven weeks collecting, editing, pairing, and publishing ninety-nine pieces from English-language writers across Quebec, writing about their experiences of the pandemic. Which makes all of this rather meta, I suppose—writing about lying in bed thinking about what I'll write.

Last night, I read back over the articles—the range of stories, voices, and lives. Intimate glimpses into anxiety and fear. Grief, love, generosity, and courage. The feeling of community, of views and comments growing as the weeks went on, of people thanking each other for sharing their experiences. Remarking on resonances. Wishing each other luck. The sense of time passing.

There was snow on the ground when this began, and all this—this COVID-19—seemed unbelievable. The next few days are due to be hot. Today, Montreal will finally re-open, albeit in limited ways. Shops but not schools. Workplaces but not theatres or cafes, clubs or bars.

When this began, it seemed unbelievable that there would not soon be a definite "after." When everything would return to normal, and we could have a jolly good session hugging and crying into each other's faces. Now, as the sense of a "new normal" extends indefinitely and uncertainly, it feels more accurate to talk about "before" and "what now"?

No neat endings. The pale time brightens. The stories remain.

Afterword

· · · · · · · · ·

CRYSTAL CHAN

Ever since I learned to write, I've struggled to chronicle my days. When I was six or seven, my mother took me to the dollar store and let me choose a notebook. Every year, I'd begin recording what I did in a new notebook, full of ambition, but I always gave up eventually. While I loved it, I felt like the odd one out, wanting to be separated from the other children at play. As an adult, I felt the same guilt and tug toward more useful, helpful responsibilities. Sitting down with pen and paper seemed like an indulgent escape from other people, from life. How could reading and scribbling alone help others?

Then COVID-19 struck. In March 2020, I quarantined myself to avoid risk. I bought six weeks of groceries and only left home to walk the quietest side streets, avoiding even the alley cats that came purring. For an introvert, quarantine felt like a Grimm fairy tale. I used to long for more alone time, but now I felt cursed by too much isolation. I am a writer, so every day should have been an artist's retreat. Instead, I simply retreated.

I read a lot of news, then I stopped reading altogether. The virus controlled what happened. What could I do? The way to play my part was to stay home, do nothing. I hid in bed. I abandoned my calendar, my notebook. I stopped writing. Anyway, nothing much happened that seemed worth writing about. I slept, ate, worked.

One of my jobs is editing an online column for the Quebec Writers' Federation. In late March, the Executive Director, Lori Schubert, reached out to me with an idea from board member Elise Moser; on the column website, we could create a venue for pieces by people documenting a day in their life under COVID restrictions.

Rachel McCrum would solicit submissions. I was asked to help with publishing these daily chronicles. We released the first piece on April 6.

Over the next few weeks, we received a deluge of responses. Suddenly, I was forced to read again. I read about working the evening shift at the ER. I read about racist street hecklers, attending school online, insomnia, haircuts—about discovering you might be the first Canadian case of COVID-19. The writers were hungry and cheerful and bored and horny. They were grieving. Living. Some couldn't find a scrap of time without interruption from the dogs, the caregiver, the adult daughter that had moved back in. Some dreamed of a quiet room; another bemoaned the isolation of living in a new city without any friends, and saw the same quiet room as a trap.

I had given up writing because my days just didn't seem important, especially during a global pandemic. Reading these essays, peeking into a variety of other people's days, I realized there was no right way to act. I was struck by a common refrain: at the very least, writing about their day gave people a feeling of control.

As I began reading the chronicles, I started writing again. Inspired, I dug out a spiral notebook and chronicled my own days. And the more I wrote, the more I felt connected to others. Social distancing had forced all of us into sitting alone indoors, but writing was one of those few acts that could be done alone and then shared with others. Without leaving my computer, I could read and write. I could inform myself through community action boards, update and circulate resources, and assist by volunteering, organizing. My notebook wasn't an indulgence, but a first step to witness, testify, act. Yes, it all felt like trying to clean a window when the dirt was on the other side of the pane—everything done by proxy. It never seemed like enough. But I could help instead of hide.

In the Chinese lunar calendar, there are leap months instead of leap days. In 2020, the month of April happened twice—under lockdown, a Groundhog Day time warp. The repeat month started just as the last of these chronicles were published. The first day felt like a re-set, an invitation: How would I re-live this bonus time?

I had regained power by first deciding what I took away from my day, controlling how I order the chaos around me on the page. Daily life is just a series of actions, and writing is an act, rather than a retreat from the rest of my life. I need to take action. I need solidarity. And I need to write.

Contributors

MARIANNE ACKERMAN is a playwright, novelist, and journalist. Her most recent book *Triplex Nervosa Trilogy* was published by Guernica Editions in the spring of 2020.

NOAH ALLISON is an urban and social researcher currently based in Los Angeles, where he is completing his PhD dissertation.

ANITA ANAND is a teacher, translator, and writer. She is the author of the collection *Swing in the House and Other Stories*. Her novel *A Convergence of Solitudes* will be published by Book*Hug some time in the next couple of years.

A graduate of the Comparative Canadian Literature Ph.D. program at the Université de Sherbrooke, **MICHELLE ARISS** founded the Morris House Reading Series at Bishop's University in 2004. Directed by Dr. Linda M. Morra since 2008, the QWF-supported series hosted Anakana Schofield and Kim Thúy in 2019.

ROKSANA BAHRAMITASH earned a Ph.D. from McGill after immigrating from Iran in the aftermath of the Iranian revolution and Iran-Iraq war. The author of several books and articles, she is the recipient of a Canada Council for the Arts award to write her memoirs.

LEA BEDDIA is a writer and high-school English teacher born in Montreal. She spends her time in quarantine writing young-adult fiction and building with Legos with her three children or swimming in the lake near her home in the country.

TANYA BELLEHUMEUR-ALLATT's stories, poems, and essays have been published in *Best Canadian Essays 2019* and *Best Canadian Essays 2015, The Antigonish Review, EVENT, Prairie Fire, Malahat Review, carte blanche,* and *Room.* Tanya has been nominated for both a National Magazine Award and a Western Magazine Award.

RACHEL BERGER is a parent of twins, a historian of the body, a writer of things, and a lover of walks. She lives and teaches in Tiohtià:ke/ Montreal.

SYLWIA BIELEC is a dancer, poet, mom, and instructional designer who lives and works in Montreal. Inspired by the ways we connect and disconnect—from each other, from places—Sylwia writes about the moment slowed down. She has always craved a sense of place.

JOE BONGIORNO is a writer of fiction and non-fiction. His writing has appeared in publications including *CBC, Geist, EVENT,* and *The Antigonish Review.* He won *EVENT*'s 2019 Speculative Writing Contest. He is currently working on a novel as well as a short story collection.

RANA BOSE has written twelve plays, three novels, countless poems and essays, and is a semi-retired professional engineer and one of the editors of *Montreal Serai.*

AMI SANDS BRODOFF is the award-winning author of three novels and two volumes of stories. Her novel-in-stories, *The Sleep of Apples,* is forthcoming. Ami is a participating writer in StoryScaping, a new QWF program offering creative-writing workshops to teens and seniors in underserved areas of Quebec.

Originally from the UK, EMILY BROWN has lived in Montreal for the past seven years. Although trained as a biologist, Emily has always loved to write, and has had short pieces published in the *Times Higher Education* and *The Huffington Post,* among others.

BRIAN CAMPBELL's poetry collections include *Shimmer Report* and *Passenger Flight*. Also a singer-songwriter and photographer, he runs Sky of Ink Press, which publishes chapbooks by emerging writers, and co-hosts/organizes the lawn chair soirée, a Montreal reading series. His latest EP is *On This Shore*.

LOUISE CARSON has published eleven books, two of them in 2020: *Dog Poems*, and her latest mystery, *The Cat Possessed*. Her historical novel *In Which* was shortlisted for a Quebec Writers' Federation award in 2019. With her daughter and pets, Louise lives near Montreal.

BABSIE CHALIFOUX-REIS is a Concordia University graduate in English Literature and an aspiring author. She worked as a flight attendant for a major Canadian airline for the past twelve years and is currently waiting for a callback from her layoff due to the COVID-19 pandemic.

CRYSTAL CHAN is a writer, journalist, and editor who sits on the Board of Directors of the Quebec Writers' Federation. A former Writer-in-Residence at the Banff Centre for Arts and Creativity, she is an Editor at UBC Press and is scripting and directing a CBC podcast.

CLARE CHODOS-IRVINE was raised in Seattle and London and now lives in Montreal. She is currently studying English and Creative Writing at Concordia University, and is the co-editor-in-chief of *Soliloquies Anthology*. You can Google her, but she rarely updates her blog.

MORGAN COHEN has a B.A in English Literature and is currently pursuing an M.A in Rhetoric. She likes mooing at cows and other ruminants and reading literary theory, which may initially confuse her, but leads to the contemplation and critique of the world she inhabits.

NISHA COLEMAN is the author of the memoir *Busker: Stories from the Streets of Paris* (2016). Her storytelling show, *Self-Exile*, won Best English Production at the Montreal Fringe. She is a co-producer at

Confabulation, Montreal's monthly storytelling series, as well as its French equivalent, *Enfabulation*.

TIFFANY CROTOGINO's primary goal is to make information available by translating, reporting, or otherwise documenting just about anything. She has worked on subjects ranging from the use of kaolin in papermaking to washing instructions for circus tents and policies on medical aid in dying.

DAN DAVID is a recovering journalist. He's Mohawk, and won some awards for his work. He describes himself as a genetically-engineered troublemaker thanks to his parents and ancestors. Dan bakes bread when he's not on his bicycle around Kanehsatake (not Oka) in southern Quebec.

JENNIFER DELESKIE lives in Montreal, where she is currently editing her first novel, a science fiction coming-of-age story called *Everclear*. She left the practice of law in exchange for the glamorous life of a laundress, short-order cook, and cat therapist. Jennifer grows tomatoes in her spare time.

SUSAN DOHERTY has worked at *Maclean's Magazine*, and the *International Herald Tribune* and ran an advertising production company for twenty years. Research for her debut novel, *A Secret Music*, led to ten years as a volunteer with people suffering from extreme psychosis. *The Ghost Garden* is the culmination of her work in the excavation of mental illness.

JOCELYNE DUBOIS' novel, *World of Glass*, was a finalist for the QWF's Paragraphe Hugh MacLennan Prize for Fiction. Her short stories and poetry have appeared in many reviews. Also a visual artist, Jocelyne has exhibited in Montreal galleries. A book of doodle self-portraits, *Doodling Moods,* was recently published by Sky of Ink Press.

DENISE DUGUAY is a poet, TV critic, and journalist who covered politics and business in Manitoba. While an editor at the *Montreal Gazette* (1998-2020), she launched d2tv.wordpress.com and eleventhavenue.wordpress.com and performed onstage at Words & Music, the lawn chair soirée, and Twigs & Leaves.

GEOFFREY EDWARDS, based in Quebec City, is catching his second breath as a writer after a successful career as a research scientist. His first novel, *Plenum: The First Book of Deo*, is slated for publication in 2021. He is also an editor for *Metapsychosis*.

ENDRE FARKAS, poet, playwright, and fiction author, has published eleven books of poetry, and two novels. His work has been translated into French, Spanish, Italian, Hungarian, Slovenian, and Turkish. His videopoems have been shown at festivals in Berlin, England, Greece, and the USA.

APRIL FORD is a Montreal queer writer. Their books include *Carousel*—a novel, winner of the 2020 International Book Awards for LGBTQ Fiction; *Death Is a Side-Effect*—poems; and *The Poor Children*—stories. April is the recipient of a 2016 Pushcart Prize for their short story "Project Fumarase."

MARK FOSS is the author of two novels and a collection of short stories. His words have also appeared in journals such as *The New Quarterly, subTerrain, Numéro Cinq*, and *carte blanche*. Visit him at www.markfoss.ca.

ARIELA FREEDMAN is the author of the award-winning *Arabic for Beginners* (LLP, 2017) and *A Joy to be Hidden* (LLP, 2019). She shelters in place in Montreal while dreaming of travel and working on her third novel.

Born in rural Quebec in a French-speaking household, LISANNE GAMELIN spent most of her twenties travelling, bouncing from one job to another. Then, she went to Louisiana, inspiring her to write a novel (unpublished). The first chapter appears in *Résonance* (University of Maine), 2020 edition.

CHARLES GEDEON is a creative director and interaction designer. He co-founded the media literacy platform ThinkFirst News and lectures at Concordia University. His work can be found on charliegedeon.com. Charlie is fascinated by informal learning, speculative technology, and stories from his Middle-Eastern heritage.

ELIZABETH GLENN-COPELAND is a multi-disciplinary artist whose writing has appeared in *Resilience Magazine, Deep Times Journal,* and *Forge Journal,* among others. She wrote *Daring to Hope at the Cliff's Edge: Pangea's Dream Remembered,* after two years of communing with three-hundred-million-year-old rock.

MURIEL GOLD POOLE, C.M, Ph.D. is a producer/director, Quebec theatre historian, former artistic director of the Saidye Bronfman Centre Theatre, and the author of seven books. Her multicultural policies and her commitment to staging Canadian plays, among other things, led to her appointment in 2007 as a member of the Order of Canada.

JILL GOLDBERG wrote and co-produced the short film, *Homeland,* which has been viewed at festivals around North America and Europe. From within her pandemic bubble, Jill writes, teaches literature and creative writing, and dreams of the day she can return to dancing the tango.

DIDI GORMAN writes blogs, columns, essays, and short fiction. Her writing covers various subjects, such as health food, social issues, community, environment, wellbeing, and humour. Her works regularly appear in *The Townships Sun, The Record,* and *Wise Choice Market*'s blog. She lives in Sherbrooke, Quebec.

Montrealer **JOANNE GORMLEY** has worked as a theatre artist, a teacher of ESL to immigrants and refugees, and in the field of mental health. As a retired yoga-studio owner, she now devotes more time to writing fiction and memoir.

Co-director of Guernica Editions, **CONNIE GUZZO-MCPARLAND** holds a BA in Italian Literature and an MA in Creative Writing from Concordia University. She has published two novels: *The Girls of Piazza d'Amore* (Linda Leith Publishing), shortlisted for QWF's Concordia University First Book Prize, and *The Women of Saturn* (Inanna Publications).

BRENDA HARTWELL is a writer and editor based in Quebec's Eastern Townships. She is editor-in-chief of the *Taproot* anthology series and has been a member of TILT, an Amherst-style writing group, for many years. She recently completed her first novel.

KATE HENDERSON lives, works, and writes in Verdun, Quebec, where she walks along the river every morning. She has moved to a new apartment and heat-treated all of her belongings. She is grateful for the always-changing current.

LOUISE HINTON is a writer and translator living in Montreal. She grew up in a small English-speaking community in Quebec City. She has collaborated on a number of translations from French to English, including a novel, *Bolero*, by Assar Santana.

JONATHAN KAPLANSKY works as a literary translator of French in Montreal. He won a French Voices Award to translate Annie Ernaux's *Things Seen* (*La vie extérieure*). His most recent translation is Jean-Pierre Le Glaunec's *The Cry of Vertières: Liberation, Memory, and the Beginning of Haiti*.

CAROL KATZ has two published books: a children's book, *Zaidie and Ferdele: Memories of My Childhood*, and a graphic novel, *Mad or Bad: The Story of My Grandmother*. Several of Carol's poems and short stories have been published in journals and anthologies in Canada and the United States.

BARBARA KELLY is a theatre educator who taught at Dawson College, where she directed many plays. She has also co-produced two of her own plays. She holds master's degrees in English and Theatre. She lives in the Laurentians, where she hikes, skis, and writes poetry.

ANGELA LEUCK is the author of four poetry collections and editor of numerous anthologies, the latest of which is *Water Lines: New Writing from the Eastern Townships of Quebec* (Studio Georgeville, 2019). She lives in Hatley, Quebec.

In her work, **ANNE LEWIS** mines the beauty of being human and the power of inner wisdom. An award-winning journalist for over thirty years, Anne returned to personal writing for healing after a car accident in Rome. She was born in Belfast, N. Ireland.

ANN LLOYD was born in Wales and has written for leading UK women's magazines as well as Canadian ad agencies. The author of *Lurching into the Looney Bin* and *Geriatric Erotica: The Oxymoron* and plays accepted by the CBC, she spends her time lecturing and running writing workshops.

FRANCESCA M. LODICO is a writer and editor in Montreal. Her work has appeared in *PEN International*, *Canadian Geographic*, *enRoute* and *Maisonneuve*, and been broadcast on CBC Radio. She won the *Accenti* Magazine Award and has been shortlisted for the F.G. Bressani Literary Prize.

Based in Quebec City, **NORA LORETO** is the author of *Take Back the Fight: Organizing Feminism for the Digital Age* (Fernwood, 2020) and the editor of the *Canadian Association of Labour Media*. Nora co-hosts the popular podcast *Sandy and Nora Talk Politics* with Sandy Hudson.

AIMEE LOUW is a writer whose work incorporates disability justice with flourishing futures. Her award-nominated debut poetry book, *Less Sweet than Chocolate or Concrete*, is out now with Metonymy Press. Twitter connect: @aimeeiswriting.

DORU LUPEANU is a Marketing Director working for an educational technology company in Montreal, Canada. Originally from Romania, he is currently working on his first science-fiction novel building on his experience as a journalist and short movie scriptwriter.

JEFFREY MACKIE-DEERNSTED is a poet whose work has been published both nationally and internationally. He was a long-time figure on the Montreal literary scene and hosted the popular *Literary Report* on CKUT Radio. Mackie is now serving as an Anglican minister in Dawson City, Yukon.

ALEXANDRE MARCEAU is the Co-Founder of and Fiction Editor for *yolk*. At Bishop's University, he was the Opinions Editor for and published in the *Campus Newspaper*, had work printed in *The Mitre*, and perused the university's literary archive for a research project. He is in Scotland, completing his Masters at the University of Edinburgh.

MAUREEN MAROVITCH is a TV writer, director, and producer. She shares a home in Lachine with two mostly delightful teens, a supportive husband, and a patient dog. She's nearly completed her first YA novel, and loves being able to write that phrase.

ILONA MARTONFI is an editor, poet, and activist. The most recent of her four poetry collections is *Salt Bride* (Inanna, 2019); *The Tempest* (Inanna, 2022) is forthcoming. The author of six chapbooks, Ilona is Curator of Visual Arts Centre and Argo Bookshop Reading Series and won the QWF 2010 Community Award.

RACHEL MCCRUM is a poet, performer, event organizer, and workshop facilitator. Originally from Northern Ireland, she published her first collection of poetry *The First Blast to Awaken Women Degenerate* in Scotland in 2016. She has been living in Montreal since 2017.

GREGORY MCKENZIE is an American-born, Montreal-based translator. He holds degrees in literature from Université du Quebec à Montreal and in translation from McGill University. He is a speaker of four languages. As a confirmed homebody, he feels he should have been more prepared for the current situation.

LIS MCLOUGHLIN, Ph.D., is a land advocate and writer whose non-academic work has appeared in *Tributaries, Stonewalls II*, and *The Ecological Citizen*. She lives off-grid in Northfield, Massachusetts, and in a stone structure in Montreal, Quebec.

CURTIS MCRAE's fiction has appeared in *Soliloquies Anthology*. He has worked as a journalist for Blue Metropolis and was a finalist in the 2019 QWF Prize for Young Writers. Curtis began work on his MA in Creative Writing at Concordia University in the Fall of 2020.

Writer and visual artist AUDREY MEUBUS has written for television and film, including the short film *Family Feast* (dir. Rémi Fréchette) which represented Canada in the international horror anthology *Deathcember* (2019). She is working on her first book and a script for a feature-length film.

STEPHANIE MOLL moved to Montreal in 2018 from Austin, Texas. She is enjoying retirement by exploring her new surroundings and making new friends. Her writing experience consists of a blog that she started when she moved. Y'all feel free to follow her adventures at Chez-new.blogspot.com.

LINDA M. MORRA is the former Craig Dobbin Chair (UCD, Ireland, 2016-2017) whose book, *Unarrested Archives*, was a finalist for the Gabrielle Roy Prize in English in 2015. Her edition of Jane Rule's *Taking My Life* was shortlisted for the LAMBDA in 2012.

REBECCA MORRIS is an award-winning Montreal writer. Her fiction has appeared in the *Malahat Review*, *Prairie Fire*, *carte blanche*, *FreeFall* and elsewhere. She is working on a collection of short stories as well as a #metoo novel set in her hometown of Guelph, Ontario.

TIMOTHY NIEDERMANN has written a novel, *Wall of Dust*, and is currently the Editor of *Silver Sage* magazine, an internet publication for people over 40. He is a regular reviewer for the *Ottawa Review of Books* and has published in *The Montreal Review*.

KAREN ISABEL OCAÑA is a Montreal-based writer and translator. She was shortlisted in 2017 for the QWF Cole Foundation Prize for Translation for *Rooms*, her translation of Louise Dupré's poetry collection *Chambres*. She belongs to the Literary Translators' Association of Canada and the Quebec Writers' Federation.

JIM OLWELL has published two chapbooks of poetry, *Crossings* and *Pensions*; and a memoir of the Viet-Nam War era, *The Luck of the Draw*. He co-founded the "Speakup" reading series. He's working on a memoir of organizing NYC's Irish Arts Center from 1972-78.

DEBORAH OSTROVSKY is a writer, editor, and translator living in Montreal. Her work has appeared in many Canadian magazines and journals. She has received the Barbara Deming Memorial Fund and the Marian Hebb Research Grant from the Access Copyright Foundation.

SOPHIE PAGÉ is a business assistant by day and a writer by night. She holds a BA in Creative Writing from Concordia University and an MA in Library and Information Science from McGill. She lives in Montreal with her cat and an abundance of books.

Retired from careers in international development and immigration law, MIRIAM S. PAL has recently completed a memoir *Ballet is Not for Muslim Girls*. Her essays have been published in, among others, *The Globe and Mail*, the *Montreal Gazette* and *The Times* of India.

ALISON PIPER is a Montreal-based writer, editor, and instructional designer, who develops training and marketing materials for various clients. She has written and edited several educational and business books. A member of the Quebec Writers' Federation, she enjoys writing short fiction as a hobby.

CONSTANTIN POLYCHRONAKOS is professor in Pediatrics and Human Genetics at the McGill University Health Centre. He spends part of his professional time in China, where he is honourary professor at the Zhejiang University Children's Hospital and chief scientific officer of MaiDa Inc., a genetic-testing company.

RITA POMADE is a two-time award winner at the Moondance International Film Festival for a script and a short story. Her work has appeared in various anthologies, and her travel memoir, *Seeker: A Sea Odyssey*, was shortlisted for QWF's 2019 Concordia University First Book Prize.

JOSH QUIRION is a French-Canadian writer from a small rural municipality in the Eastern Townships of Quebec, Canada. He is a graduate of Concordia University's M.A. program in Creative Writing and Editor-in-Chief of the Montreal-based publication, *yolk*. Quirion writes and resides in Montreal.

KENNETH RADU is a two-time winner of QWF awards for best English-language Quebec fiction and a nominee for a Governor-General's award. His latest book is *Net Worth*, published by DC Books. He lives in rural Quebec and has recently completed a manuscript of linked stories.

Montreal-borN **CAROLYNN RAFMAN** has lived in different corners of our island. Since retiring from McGill, she lives closer to the St. Lawrence River to enjoy watching the seasons change. Kate and Patricia, her daughters, are always in her heart and mind as she writes.

HARRY RAJCHGOT is a member of the Greene Writers Collective, and Ilona Martonfi's Rue Towers Writers. He is the author of the novel *Gravitational Fields, Purimspiel!*, and *The Sweetness of Life,* a family memoir. He is managing editor of *JONAHmagazine.*

MARIAN REBEIRO is a cultural worker currently based in Montreal. With a background in art education and film production, she continues to pursue her passion for fostering inclusive and representative creative spaces while working with the QWF. Marian thoroughly enjoys a good origin story.

At 57, **WENDY REICHENTAL** found her footing and started her new career as a reflexologist. Wendy enjoys writing about life's foibles. She has always been a homebody and espouses Larry David's sentiment: "Nothing good ever happens going out of the house."

A former European circus tramp schooled in elephants, **BYRON REMPEL** also moonlights as a writer and is the author of four books. He currently lives with his wife Geneviève and their dog Bibi-Luv on a ranch in the Laurentians, where he is writing about Africa.

GINA ROITMAN is the author of a short-story collection, *Tell Me A Story, Tell Me the Truth,* and a biography, *Midway to China and Beyond.* Her work has aired on CBC Radio and appeared in two anthologies, *The New Spice Box* and *Wherever I Find Myself.*

JILL LESLIE SAPPHIRE-GOLDBERG's love of words has fed her passion for translating, voracious reading, inadvertent editing, writing, and helping others find their voice. Originally from New York, she spends as much time as possible in Quebec's subarctic with the Naskapis, grateful to work in Indigenous education.

ROBERT EDISON SANDIFORD is the award-winning author of *And Sometimes They Fly*, *The Tree of Youth*, *Sand for Snow*, and *Attractive Forces*. With the poet Linda M. Deane, he produces the arts and culture forum artsetcbarbados.com. His latest book is *Fairfield* (dcbooks.ca).

GREG SANTOS is the author of *Blackbirds* (2018), *Rabbit Punch!* (2014), and *The Emperor's Sofa* (2010). His latest poetry collection with DC Books, *Ghost Face*, was published in the fall of 2020. Santos is the Editor-in-Chief of *carte blanche* magazine. He lives in Montreal with his wife and two children.

IAN THOMAS SHAW is a novelist and translator. His first novel, *Soldier, Lily, Peace and Pearls,* was published by Deux Voiliers Publishing (2011) and his second novel, *Quill of the Dove*, by Guernica Editions (2019). He is the founder of the *Ottawa Review of Books*.

ROMY SHILLER is a pop culture expert and one of Canada's leading underground artistic and academic voices in gender fluidity. She holds a Ph.D. in Drama from the University of Toronto and specializes in Gender and Film. She lives in Montreal, where she continues her writing.

SIVAN SLAPAK works in Montreal's arts and culture sector, and toward completing a collection of interlinked short stories. Some of her writing can be found in *The New Quarterly*, *Montréal Serai*, *carte blanche*, and an anthology published by *Véhicule Press*.

SU J SOKOL is a social rights advocate and a writer of interstitial fiction. Sokol is the author of three novels: *Cycling to Asylum* (Deux Voiliers Publishing 2014), *Run J Run* (Renaissance Press 2019), and *Zee* (Bouton d'or Acadie 2020). Sokol's short fiction has appeared in various magazines and anthologies.

BERNICE ANGELINE SORGE is a visual artist and poet. Her art has been exhibited in different cities of the world and is in the collections of the BAnQ, Cirque du Soleil, and Loto Quebec, among others. Her writing appears in the recent anthology *Waterlines*.

CAROLYN MARIE SOUAID is the Montreal-based author of eight poetry collections and the acclaimed novel *Yasmeen Haddad Loves Joanasi Maqaittik* (Baraka Books, 2017). She has performed at festivals and literary events in Canada and abroad, and her work has been featured on CBC-Radio.

ANDI STEWART is a writer and artist based in Montreal. He's been published with *yolk*, *Graphite* and other local magazines. You can find him and his work on Instagram at @_andi_stewart. He graduated with an MA in Theatre from East15 in London, UK.

SUREHKA SURENDRAN was born in Montreal to immigrants of Sri Lankan Tamil origin. In 2017, she graduated from Université du Québec en Outaouais and she became a nurse clinician. She is now working as an emergency room nurse at the Cité-de-la-Santé Hospital in Laval.

SHELLEY TEPPERMAN is a multilingual writer and filmmaker based in Montreal who collaborates as a director, story editor, and consultant on documentary and dramatic films and on television series. Her current film is set in a disappearing Sicilian village. (More information at www.shelleytepperman.ca).

MARY THALER lives in Quebec City, where she works as a writer and an environmental microbiologist. She writes the webcomic *Boghaunter* and is currently revising the manuscript of a historical novel drawing on her experiences on Arctic expeditions. You can find her writing at marythaler.wordpress.com.

LINDA THOMPSON knew in grade school that writing would play an important part in her life. While others groaned when a composition was assigned, she was already writing the story in her mind. Today, her writing is inspired by life, memories, and interesting people.

CAROLE THORPE's portfolio includes writing, visual arts, printmaking, and glassblowing. She studied printmaking at the Alberta College of Art and Design and English at the University of Calgary. Her work has been published in *Tessera*, *Open Letter*, *West Coast Line*, *blue buffalo*, *absinthe*, among others. Born in Montreal, she returned east in 2010.

MARIE TULLY's poetry and prose comment on a life well-lived, on people and places that have impacted her, favourably or otherwise. When not occupied with finishing her first novel, she can be found in the gardens of her home in the Eastern Townships.

KARIN TURKINGTON has lived in Montreal for four years, having moved from Southern Ontario. She began writing a legal memoir just prior to moving to Montreal and has now completed it. She loves to sing and write poetry and has written a few children's songs.

JIM UPTON lives in Montreal. He is the author of *Maker*, a novel to be published by Baraka Books in the fall of this year.

CAROLYNE VAN DER MEER lives and writes in Montreal, Canada. She has two published books, *Motherlode: A Mosaic of Dutch Wartime Experience* and *Journeywoman*. A collection of poetry about Marguerite Bourgeoys was published by Guernica in 2020. Her poetry and prose have been published internationally.

CAROLINE VU is the author of two novels: *Palawan Story* and *That Summer in Provincetown*. Both have been translated into French. *Palawan Story* won the 2016 Canadian Authors Association's Fred Kerner Award. It was shortlisted for QWF's 2014 Concordia University First Book Prize.

AMIE WATSON is a Montreal-based writer and journalist. Her work has appeared in *The Globe & Mail*, *National Geographic Traveller UK*, *enRoute*, and the *Montreal Gazette*. When not writing, she's usually pickling something.

ELISA ROBIN WELLS was born and raised in Montreal. She has a degree in English Literature from McGill University and in Fashion Design from F.I.T. in NYC. Since returning to Montreal, Elisa has been publishing articles, working on her memoir, and participating in creative writing salons.

DANIELLE WONG is the author of *Bubble Fusion*, a collection of poems about raising a child with autism. Her work has appeared in *Soft Cartel*, *Montreal Writes*, *Tipton Poetry*, *The Daily Drunk*, and *Kalopsia Lit*, as well as in various anthologies. She enjoys losing herself in forests.

JOEL YANOFSKY (26 September 1955 – 23 December 2020) was a freelance writer and author of six books and two plays. He won two National Magazine Awards. His memoirs *Mordecai & Me: An Appreciation of a Kind* and *Bad Animals: A Father's Accidental Education in Autism* both won QWF's Mavis Gallant Prize for Non-fiction.

ANABELLE ZALUSKI grew up in Toronto and is now based in Montreal. She enjoys tiny versions of normal things, and hates cilantro. Her work has been published in *Montreal Writes*, *HerStry*, *yolk*, and *Marias at Sampaguitas*, among others. She was previously the Editor-in-Chief at *Soliloquies Anthology*.

KAREN ZEY is from *la belle ville de* Pointe-Claire, Quebec. Her creative nonfiction stories and craft essays have appeared in various literary journals. Karen leads Circle of Life Writers' workshops at her community library. You can read more of her work at www.karenzey.com.

 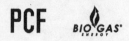